Dear Stevie, I love you.

And there's the point of the letter I never finished last night, Stevie. I'll write it again, since I can't ever say it out loud, can't ever say it straight out to your face, no matter how much I dream of it.

Dear, dear Stevie, dearest Stephan, I love you.

And now that I've written that, now that I've—in your phrase—come to the point, I don't want to write anything else. Good night, Stevie.

═══════════════════════════════════

NORMA FOX MAZER is the author of many well-known books for young adults, including *Someone to Love; Up in Seth's Room; Dear Bill, Remember Me?; Saturday, the Twelfth of October;* and *A Figure of Speech,* all available in Dell Laurel-Leaf editions, and *I, Trissy,* available in a Dell Yearling edition. She lives in Jamesville, New York.

SUMMER GIRLS, LOVE BOYS
and other short stories

Norma Fox Mazer

LAUREL-LEAF BOOKS bring together under a single imprint outstanding works of fiction and nonfiction particularly suitable for
young adult readers, both in and out of the classroom. Charles F.
Reasoner, Professor Emeritus of Children's Literature and Reading, New York University, is consultant to this series.

Published by
Dell Publishing
a division of
Bantam Doubleday Dell Publishing Group, Inc.
666 Fifth Avenue
New York, New York 10103

ISBN: 0-440-98375-4

RL: 5.1

Reprinted by arrangement with Delacorte Press

Printed in the United States of America

One Previous Edition

May 1989

10 9 8 7 6 5 4 3 2 1

KRI

This book is in memory of my father.
He lived his life among women:
mother, sisters, wife, daughters.
To them all he was fiercely
loyal and devoted.

"Why, Sir," said Lucy. "I think—I don't know—but I think I could be brave enough."

C. S. LEWIS

The Lion, The Witch, and The Wardrobe

Contents

Mother/Daughter Song

(O my darling, O my daughter, O my dear. Life is short, life is long. Life is sad, life is sweet. O my daughter, O my darling, O my dear.)

> At 14, she raged
> At 16, vowed she would
> At 17, wondered if she could.

(O my darling, O my daughter, O my dear.)

> At 20, she yearned
> At 22, she learned
> At 23, almost free.

(O my darling, O my daughter, O my dear.)

At 25, she found another
At 27, became a mother
At 28, began the song.

(O my darling, O my daughter, O my dear. Life is short, life is long. Life is sad, life is sweet. O my daughter, O my darling, O my dear.)

Avie Loves Ric Forever

Dear Stephan,

Although you don't know it, this is the 25th letter I've written you. Yes! 25 letters which you've never received. I can see your eyes turning dark with greed for those 25 letters. And long ones, too! I find it a real pain to write an English theme, but when I sit here at my desk in the little cubbyhole in my room and write you a letter, it's entirely different. I go on for page after page. And each time I feel better for it, too—for a little while, anyway, until the sadness comes back.

The sadness of knowing I'm writing to you, dear Stephan, but that you'll never read my letter. And, oh, how I wish you could. Selfishly, I wish it, for me, because then you would know my deepest feelings. But there's even another reason, and that's that you're always so pleased, almost triumphant, when you get mail. Aha! A letter! You hold it up, waving it like a flag. I've seen you do it a hundred times. As for me, I'd a thousand times rather have a real face-to-face conversation. Or, second best, a good long talk on the phone.

Are you wondering, if that's the case—and considering that I not only see you every day, but could pick up the phone anytime and call you—why it is I've written you 24 letters and am writing you a twenty-fifth? And none of which you'll ever receive? A mystery, Stephan!

Once you said to me, "Richie, how can you read all those junky mysteries?" I was more than a little bit annoyed, if you remember, and told you I didn't see how *you* could read all that junky science-fiction stuff.

"At least there's some semblance of thought in them," you said in your snottiest professor voice. To make peace we finally agreed to forever disagree about our reading. As if that were the only thing we disagreed on! I could make up a list of 50 things on which we have utterly opposite viewpoints. Beginning with you being a sun worshiper and going down the line through food, movies, clothes, people, politics, and if the Student Council has any real influence. (I vote yes, you, no.)

And another thing we disagree on—you like to get straight to the point. In fact, it's one of your favorite sayings: "Get to the point, Richie!" Whereas I like nothing so much as to ramble, to get in all the little interesting details. And don't deny, my dear best friend, that there have been plenty of times when you've listened to my rambling stories and enjoyed yourself like anything.

You even said it last year when we did our camping weekend. "What would these couple of days be like, Richie, without your endless stories?"

I wasn't too pleased about that "endless" but you insisted you meant it as a compliment and told me about Scheherazade, who saved her life, night after night, by telling the king a story that never ended. Each evening when he might have—and indeed planned to—order her execution, instead he let her live to go on with her story the following night.

For the rest of that weekend you were Kingy and I was Zady. Stev—Stephan, do you remember? I remember nearly everything from all the good times we've had together. I know *you* remember everything you ever read and everything that has to do with school and studies. (I, as little as possible. How is it that school doesn't bore you?)

By the way, I hope you notice how carefully I'm calling you by your given name, rather than the old familiar, careless "Stevie"? It's an effort for me not to call you Stevie, but as you've made your wishes very clear . . .

"I'm 17, damn it!" you said on Saturday, "and Stevie sounds like seven." Of course, I argued with you. "No, not at all, it's your *name*." "It's a diminutive, Richie," you said. "It means *little* Steven. Who needs it?"

With that I shut up, since I'm aware you're more than a bit sensitive about your height. Not that you're short. Good grief, Stephan, five six is hardly short. But, yes, I know, when your father is nearly six feet and your brother as well, and then, to make matters worse—*me*, being six feet and even a bit more— Yes, I can understand your point of view.

Do you realize, Stephan, that hardly ever a week passes, for me, without some cheerful idiot asking me how the air is up here? Or if, since my ear is so close to God's mouth, I would be so good as to give a weather forecast? And since I'm on the subject of my being so tall, let me congratulate you on being the one person in the entire world who has never felt called upon to comment. And this includes my darling mother, who is always making bracing remarks to me —"Tall girls are so splendid" is her favorite, along with a jab in my lower back to make sure I'm standing straight.

Tonight, though, she got started once again about how I must, must, *must* keep up my marks if I want to go to college.

I do believe if I hear the word *underachievement* one more time, I'll scream. Or else blow the damn thing up. What, you've never heard of Achievement Bridge? A great pet of the governor's—he spent millions on it. The mystery is why everyone thinks I'm under it.

Why can't they all understand that I do enough to satisfy me? I have my dreams, too—which you know—about being a marine biologist. But I don't tell them, because what a shout that would bring. You, Richie, with your so-so grades and your lazy attitude towards schoolwork!

"Look," I should tell them, "I learn what I need to, and the rest of it can go to the devil!" If they'd care to check a bit more carefully, they'd see that my marks in science, etc. are perfectly okay. It's only in subjects I don't give a hoot for that I let down. And why not? Where is it written that everyone must learn everything? "But you're capable of so much more," my mother says. And Mr. Pickering, our dear guidance man, coughs and says, "A-hem, discipline . . ." "A-hem, good study habits . . ." "A-hem, anything worth doing . . ."

All right! I did my studying tonight, and now, instead of history, I prefer to think about how next month you and I will be off again on our annual great camping weekend. Despite the fact that we've been doing it now for six years (and survived), I predict that everyone will, as usual, tell us we're mad to go camping at the end of May when there's still apt to be snow on the ground in the woods.

The very first year we made up our camping plan, we wanted to go in *March*. Naturally, our parents objected. We'd freeze our tender little bums! We'd catch cold! We'd be shivering mummies when they came to fetch us! Our three parents were united, and against *us*! A gang-up, we called it, but since we were only 11, we caved in. We didn't go camping until May, and ever since, each year on Memorial Day weekend—

All right! I can almost hear you clearing your throat, which also says, as clearly as words, "Richie, get to the point."

The point being—why have I written you 24, and now a 25th letter?

To begin with, I've told you all this before in at least a dozen of those undelivered letters, but I'll do it once again. And, furthermore, after explaining myself, I'm determined to think seriously about sending you this letter, rather than locking it away in my desk with all the others.

Does that, too, sound rather strange? *Send* the letter? Go to all the trouble of going down the block and dropping it in the corner mailbox, thereby running the risk of its being lost by the Pony Express and never being delivered? All that, when I could simply cut across our lawn, leap that anemic hedge my mother planted, and slip the letter safely into the metal slot in your front door?

No, Stevie, if I do get up the nerve to deliver this letter to you, it will be done properly through the United States Mail, simply because that way I might be on hand when you pick up the envelope. I might be right there the moment you whistle through your teeth with pleasure at having received a letter. "Who can it be from?" you'll say, turning it over and over. You won't want to open it at once (the way I would);

instead you'll hold it up to the light (will you recognize my big, sloppy handwriting?), scrutinize the postmark —in a word, take your time with it (as you do with nearly everything), while I'll be trembling in every limb with impatience.

It's maddening how you make everything last as long as possible! Whether it's an ice cream, a book, or a letter, you just don't let yourself gobble. You're very disciplined that way, whereas I'm lazy about such things. Once, seeing me devour my ice cream in two bites, you said, "Richie, slow down and savor things a bit!"

Yes, I want to! But I haven't yet succeeded in finding out how to do it. I'm excessive in every way. We're different, Stephan, down the line, but there's a hope in me that in one way— That's what this letter is about, that *one way*, but I can't yet bring myself to say it, flat out. Can you guess, Stevie? Please try! Here, I'll give you a hint.

It's true our personalities, our minds, our characters, are utterly different, yet we're so close that, while we each have an aura, we also have something that I call a Third Aura. You've said to me that people stare at us at times because, like Mutt and Jeff, one of us is tall and one is short, but the tallness and shortness aren't distributed the way people expect. I have a different idea, however. I think it's our Third Aura. *That's* what people notice because it's really a rare thing.

Oh, go ahead, laugh. I know you don't believe in

such things, but I do—in other lives, reincarnation, and auras. To me, it's all part of God and love and—

Dear Stephan,

I never did get a chance to finish the last letter and I've made it a rule (maybe a silly one, but as it's *my* silly rule, I try to go with it)—I've made it a rule to either finish my letter to you the same day I start it, or else begin another the next time I'm in a writing-to-Stevie mood.

And the reason for that is that what I felt yesterday I often don't feel today. Oh, no, not the important big feelings, but little feelings—moods, worries, angers, and so on. You'd be surprised how many letters I've written you out of anger. As you so rarely get angry at anyone yourself, it always takes you by surprise when I fly out.

Anyway, last night my mother came in about midnight, very surprised. "Richie, what are you sitting up so late for?" I covered the letter with my arm and mumbled something about an English paper. Of course, this was exactly the right answer. But, tonight, I've stuffed a towel under my door so the light won't show through. "Good night," my mother called, going past to her bedroom. "Good night, Mom," I said, sounding sleepy. But, in fact, I wasn't, and am not, at all sleepy. I've found out that, some nights, to be properly ready for the sandman, I first have to write you. Sometimes, just a short note, as follows:

Dear Stevie, I love you.

And there's the point of the letter I never finished last night, Stevie. I'll write it again, since I can't ever say it out loud, can't ever say it straight out to your face, no matter how much I dream of it.

Dear, dear Stevie, dearest Stephan, I love you.

And now that I've written that, now that I've—in your phrase—come to the point, I don't want to write anything else. Good night, Stevie.

Stevie!

Really, I have had it up to *here* with your Karens and Kims and Kathis. What is it with you and girls with names beginning with *K*? Do you realize that *every year* for the past two or three years you have developed at least one, sometimes two or even three, great romantic attachments? And lucky me!—I get to hear all the details. How you first noticed Kay, what it was about Kitty that electrified you, and do you think, Richie, I ought to call Karen up, or maybe it would be better to wait till we run into each other in some natural way, but on the other hand, and so on and so on . . .

I've been through all this with you enough times, Stevie, to know the whole route by heart. And I admit, until recently, I've enjoyed being your ally and confidante. Why not? I knew it would all come to nothing, most likely. And *we* would go on, just as we always had.

But now we have the latest—Katherine, if you please!—and I'm no longer so tolerant and friendly

15

about your love life, Stevie. If you only knew how much I wanted to tell you to shut up, please *shut up*, as you went on and on about Katherine Ritter today on the way to school.

Katherine, with the thick braids. Katherine, whom you suddenly adore (at a distance, of course!). And did I know Katherine (yes), the fair Katherine, the lovely Katherine? And would I, by any chance, have any classes with her? And, of course, you didn't even have to say what came next! Would I have a chance to talk to her, and, well . . . I barely listened. I knew exactly what you would ask. You never want so very much, after all—a modest request. And I've never minded helping you—just the opposite, in fact. All you ever want is a little report about your Katherine or Kim or Kay. Is she aware of you? Do you have a chance, et cetera? No more did you want today.

And as you made your damned request you had on your sweetest expression, which made me love you even more, and thus resent you beyond belief. Why should you look at me that way, when it's about another girl that you're speaking?

The hell with it, Stevie! The hell with it! I resign as your Ann Landers-in-waiting, as your loyal lieutenant, as your faithful, dumb mutt who does her duty and comes back for her reward—a pat on the head and a doggy biscuit. Go speak to your Katherine yourself!

P.S. Your timing stinks! For somebody so smart, you are incredibly dumb. Didn't you suspect even for an instant what you were doing to me? If I didn't know better, I'd accuse you of outright sadism. Do you realize you chose to tell me about this newest love of yours just as we walked toward the railroad overpass?

Do you get it now, Stevie? Such a wave of misery came over me that I couldn't even speak, and it was made all the worse as I happened to look up, just as you breathed your precious Katherine's name, and see AVIE LOVES RIC FOREVER above us on the overpass. Of course, I've seen it before! Hundreds—no, thousands of times—up there in all its ugly purple Day-Glo splendor. We've both seen it and laughed over it, and even wondered how the unknown, love-lorn Avie did the job—hanging by her toes from the bridge? Dangling from a helicopter? On top of a giant ladder?

We thought ourselves very funny, very smart, smirking together over anyone who could be so gauche and naive and silly—(antisocial, as well, we mumbled piously to each other—imagine painting slogans on public bridges! Tch! Tch!). We didn't imagine that Avie was in pain and that she did something heroic and admirable in letting the world and Ric (whoever he is—some ignorant boy who sees nothing beyond his nose, I swear!)—in letting him know what she felt in her deepest heart.

Yes, Avie, whoever you are, I salute you! I only wish I had your courage!

Dear Stevie,

Are you satisfied? Are you happy now that I've brought you news of Katherine? Nothing world-shaking, I admit, but now you know a bit more about her. She plays tennis, has two brothers, and is planning to go to Smith College. How upper upper! I slipped in that you and I were both going to State U. "I hear it's very good," she said with a sweet democratic smile.

At that moment I would gladly have stepped on one of her dainty upper-class feet—or both of them, with the passionate hope that she'd hobble for the rest of her life. I didn't tell you that, though, did I, Stevie? Nor did I tell you that your fair Katherine's sweet, sweet smile sets my teeth on edge. (I declare it as an eternal truth that girls should *never* be sweet, and boys always ought to be! Then the world might shake itself into shape.)

Furthermore, Stevie, I didn't tell you that the fair Katherine dropped a charming remark about me and my "little friend." That's you, Stephan. At that point I could have, happily, not only mashed all ten of her toes, but kicked her shins, as well.

And what else did I learn? Not too much, except that this Katherine is one of your worst-ever choices for a Crush, or a Romance, or whatever word you want to put to it. I, for one, refuse to dignify it with the word *love!* And if ever I hear that word pass your lips in regard to one of your darling Ks, Stevie, I warn you to watch out! I'm quite capable of doing something horrible.

God, Stevie! What's the matter with you? Don't you see how I feel? And why don't you feel the same for me? Maybe I should say, What's the matter with *me*? Am I too huge, too grotesque for you, Stevie? Could it really be my size that stands between us? My long legs, my tall torso, my Amazon self?

Oh, what nonsense I'm talking. So far as I know you've never had any qualms about my size. Is loving you making me ridiculous? It's true I feel off balance. I'm at a loss—I want to find a reason why you don't love me as I love you, when all the time I know these things have nothing at all to do with reason. Either you love someone, or you don't, and that's the end of it.

Oh, Stevie! I've cut myself to the heart with that statement. I see that you will never love me. How can you, when you're forever falling for dainty little Katherines? Ugh, Stevie! When I think of it, I tell myself to give up on you forever. I should, I should.

I only wish someone would tell me this—why do I have to feel this way? Why do I have to love you so much that I ache every morning waiting to see you come bounding out of your house, with your shirt bunched up and your hair wet from the shower? I tell you, it's unfair that I feel this way. And what makes it so bad—it's all one-sided.

I ask you once again: What is it? Why don't you see me? Here I am, right beneath your eyes. Well, in a manner of speaking, that is, as *you're* actually the one beneath *my* eyes. So there I am, back to that—big, oversize Richie; the monster; the giant; Richie, the freak. Yes, a freak can love someone normal, but can someone normal love a freak?

I'm going to sleep now, and I wish myself dreams that aren't about you! I need some peace! If you can't love me, then I wish you'd just get yourself out of my mind and my heart. Good night!

Salud, Stevie!

I'm in a good mood tonight, and for no other reason than it's a perfect, beautiful night. I'm sitting by my window writing, and I'm looking over at your house, and the moon is shining down on Mom's poor old hedge, and everything, somehow, seems just right. Oh, Stevie, isn't it wonderful to be alive? And today, especially, since it's exactly two months since I realized just how it was with me about you. That is, since it came to me that my feelings for you go far beyond our friendship. Oh, what a moment that was. Nothing like that had ever happened in my life, and I don't expect anything like it will ever happen again.

It wasn't exactly a light coming on in my head, nor was it like a bolt of lightning (isn't that the way these things are supposed to happen?). Instead, it was on quite an ordinary afternoon. We've been friends for so long, for years and years, and yet that one afternoon changed the entire world for me.

It was an afternoon in March when your sister asked you to take care of Anita. Remember? No, why should you? For you, it was just another time, like so many others, that you and I took the bus over to your sister's tiny pink house on Greene Street and baby-sat Anita.

You were casual that day. I, too. "Richie," you hollered under my window. "Come on down." I was downstairs already and came out the door. "Shut up, Stevie, you loudmouthed lout. What now?"

"Want to baby-sit Anita with me this afternoon?"

"Is Sharon leaving you a sinkful of dishes?" I asked.

"How can you be so suspicious?" you said. "Come on, you don't have anything better to do."

Two months ago. March 15. Ides of March. It was warm for March, you were wearing a green T-shirt that said "Turtles Love Me," and hideous magenta running shorts, which didn't at all take away from how strong and handsomely hairy your legs showed beneath them. "Is that what you're wearing?" I said.

"What's wrong with it?"

"The colors!"

But, of course, you wouldn't change, and off we went to your sister's. Oh, Stevie, isn't it strange how complicated and mixed up things can get? How hardly anything is ever just straight out? You don't want your sister's money, for instance, because you know she and Randy have so little. And, yet, she won't call you for baby-sitting if you don't let her pay you. We talked about that again on the bus. I said, "Just tell Sharon you don't want money, you don't need it, and you won't accept it."

"She says she has to pay someone," you said, "and as it's valuable work, it ought to be paid for."

There's one thing we agree on, at least—we both admire Sharon and Randy. The way they share everything—both of them going to school, both working, both taking care of Anita, and with all that, refusing to take any money from your parents.

We were talking that over just as we went into the bakery. That nice woman with the hoarse voice was there again. She always asks us questions. Are you kids new in the neighborhood? Where do you go to school? Are you brother and sister? (My least favorite question.) We've seen her before and she's struck us as a bit snoopy, but so jolly about it you can't really mind. We bought an ice cream roll and went on our way. Do you remember that ice cream roll, Stevie? I do, because it was while we were eating it—you, me, and Anita—that I *knew*.

We were in the kitchen, and you cut a slice for Anita and put it in front of her and said, "Watch it, honey, it's cold." And, somehow, the way—I don't know why, Stevie, it was such an ordinary remark—but the way you said it, sweet and loving, made me look up, look at you, and, well—yes, all of a sudden, it happened.

My heart really started pounding—just like it says in books, Stevie, and my hands got damp, and I had this painful, but somehow wonderful, jolt in my belly. And I wanted nothing more than to reach over and put my arms around you and . . . And, oh, how I wanted to touch you, Stevie, hug you, hold you, touch your hair, have you touch my hair.

Of course, we've touched! We've knocked each other around playing in the past, but this was utterly different. It took every bit of my willpower for me to sit in front of the ice cream roll and not move. I was stunned, really couldn't believe what I was feeling. You, Stevie, *you*—my best friend, my old friend, my friend-who-is-a-boy-but-not-a-boyfriend (how many times I've had to explain that to people!), and suddenly everything was upside down.

"Richie isn't eating her ice cream roll," Anita said. Her chin was smeared with chocolate.

"Oh, Richie'll eat it," you said, "and she'll eat your, too, if you're not careful, 'Nita." And you made huge gobbling noises to make her laugh. "Richie's an eating machine." Just the usual teasing about my gargantuan appetite, but it made me realize, with the most awful pain, that what I was feeling, I was feeling alone.

And now I've made myself sad, and isn't it strange? Because it's still the same wonderful night. The same moon is shining down on Mom's little hedge. Your house is still there and you inside it, and I still feel it's wonderful to be alive, but the sadness has got all mixed up with it.

Good night, Stevie. Will I ever tell you any of this?

Dear Stephan,

I use that name tonight, not out of respect for your wishes, but from a sense of formality. I feel that our relationship is changing, our friendship must take a new form. Things simply can't go on this way.

I tried to tell you that today, but you either didn't understand me, or didn't want to, or, more likely, simply weren't listening. Thinking about your newest beloved, no doubt! And that's just my point—*things cannot go on this way*. What am I, just a six-foot ear to you?

"I'm going in to play basketball," I said as we approached the Y. I was abrupt—simply veered off without another word and ran into the building, as if someone were waiting for me. In fact, the gym was empty, and I raced around like a demon for an hour, dribbling and shooting baskets until I was sweating and not thinking constantly of Stephan and his disgusting love for another girl.

This letter is *to* you, but it's *for* me. I need to get things straight in my mind. I mean to speak to you, Stevie. The question is, How much should I say? And when? And under what circumstances?

We've been friends for so long, I can't just stop seeing you (which is what I want to do) without arousing a thousand questions from everyone—my mother, your parents, your brother, and even your sister, who, the next time you go to baby-sit Anita, will be sure to say, "And where's Richie, Steve?" And then, of course, everyone in school who knows we're ancient pals, from Szasz, your dear Latin teacher, down to all our other friends. No, what a mess it will be, ending our friendship!

But I'm determined, anyway. I'm putting a stop to all this. It hurts too much to see you every day. I'm, if possible, forgetting you even exist!

Yes, I'm mad, and I'm confused and sad, too. I never knew it was possible to feel so many feelings all at once. (Mrs. Roran would hate that sentence. Every time I write, "I feel" this way, or, "I feel" that way in an English paper, she circles it in her poison green pen.)

Good night, Stevie, nothing settled.

Dear Stevie,

I've decided.

I have two choices, and I've thought about each one long and hard. The first choice is—forget you. Well, and how do I do that? Is it enough to say I will? Should I stuff my ears? Blind my eyes? Cut out my tongue?

My second choice—Drive you away. Tell you, once and for all, that I'm fed up listening to your puppy-dog slavering over other girls. "Yes," I'll say, "we've outgrown our friendship. Let's put an end to this Richie-Stevie thing. You stay on your side of the hedge, I'll stay on mine, and let's learn to get along without each other. That shouldn't be too hard for you," I'll say, making my voice as sarcastic as possible. "You have so many other interests!"

I won't give you a chance at rebuttal, Stevie. I'll say it flat out, as brutally as possible. "I'm bored with us, Stevie, let's move on to greener pastures, each of us."

I can see your face—disbelieving, at first. Is this one of Richie's dumb jokes? Gradually, you'll understand that I mean it. You'll be stunned, and then hurt. I know you, Stevie—next, a look of utter bewilderment. A look that says, But what have I done, Richie?

Now, as I write this, I see there's still another choice. The simplest way of all: Come clean. Confess. Tell the truth. Look you in the eye and say it. "Stevie, I love you." Won't that end our friendship just as effectively as anything else? And why not the truth? Should I be ashamed of what I feel? Afraid you'll laugh? Be embarrassed? Wonder what in the world you're expected to do with this soppy declaration?

Which way to go? First I think one way is the best, then the other. The fact is, I feel like the fellow in "The Lady or the Tiger." Which door to choose? But does it even matter? Because the outcome, for *me*, is always being eaten by the tiger.

But now a sneaky thought is worming its way into my mind . . . whispering in my ear. *The best way, Richie, is to tell the truth, because maybe* . . .

Maybe *what*? Aha, I see. I see the trick my mind is playing on me. Wishful thinker, Richie! Idiot, Richie! Dreaming that if I tell you I love you, Stevie, it'll jolt you awake. Jolt you into seeing *me* as I saw *you* that day in Sharon's kitchen.

I see that the one I ought to write a letter to is myself, and as follows: *Dear Richmond Parry, you fool, wake up and smell the coffee. Open your eyes. Stop dreaming. Put an end to your impossible thoughts.*

Face facts. Stephan doesn't love you. He takes you for granted. He leans on you. He uses you, and—

When I put it that way, Stevie, I see that I'm quite capable of hating you. And that's all to the good. Why should I say *anything* to you? Why give you the satisfaction of knowing I'm sick in love with you? Why allow you to laugh at me? No, this feeling of anger is so much better. Right now, as I write this, I feel strong. Yes, and I know what I'm going to do. No bleating, no mooing, no crying, just take the necessary steps. Yes, I've decided, and the verdict is—Cut you out of my life. But no speeches. Just do it. Let the facts speak for themselves. Good-bye, Stephan!

All right, Steve, you win. Once again I'm here writing to you one of my never-to-be-delivered letters. I'll begin it properly.

Dear Stevie,

This morning you came over to our house with jelly doughnuts, sat down at the kitchen table, drank three glasses of milk, and said, "Are you sick, Richie? Where were you yesterday? And the day before? What's going on? Have I done something?"

There it was—my golden opportunity to tell you our friendship was over. And I flubbed it. I said, "Uh, uh, no, no, things on my mind, mumble . . . mumble . . ."

You see, with all my fine words I turn out to be a coward. Unlike the Tin Man, I have a heart, but it's faint and timid. I'm six-feet-tall-Richmond-Parry, thought by one and all to be oh-so-tough. Old Stone

Heart, you've called me at times when movies made you cry and I sat through them dry-eyed.

You probably wouldn't believe the truth of the matter, anyway.

"You, Richie, you in love?" Old Stone Heart in love? You'd be so astonished it would pass you by, entirely, that it's YOU I'm in love with.

Oh, hell, Stevie, I give up. I'm over my craziness. I tried to convince myself I was mad at you forever, when the truth is I can *never* stay mad at you. No, not even when we've had a real fight, and that's because the next day you're always sure to show up with smiles, and your Richie-you're-not-possibly-still-mad-at-*me* looks. And, in general, succeeding so well in being sweet and humble I feel like super louse to go on being my grumbly, mean self.

This time the "fight" has happened in my head, but the effect is the same. You win. We'll stay friends. And I guess I win, too, because all of a sudden I feel happy again, and I think I know exactly what's meant by that saying, "Half a loaf is better than none."

Dear Stevie,

My last letter ever to you. I'm writing this one, as I've written so many of the others, for myself, to relieve myself of nearly unbearable feelings. I've been sitting here for hours, thinking over the weekend, and I can't yet make sense of it all. So I thought—if I put it down . . . not every detail, just the highlights . . . maybe it'll help.

We started out Saturday morning, early, on our bikes, packs on our backs, everything as fine as it could be. A 3-hour bike ride and we were at Lombard Forest. You sneezed a bit, and once a driver cut too close to me, but otherwise the trip was uneventful. Not even one of our bikes breaking down, which we've come to expect. (I had my tool kit with me.)

Then, at the forest, the usual—finding our regular camping spot (a bit disappointed to find that others had been there and left beer cans and trash). We cleaned up the site, had our lunch, and took a hike up the West Trail. Just what we've done every year. And, just as every year in the past, there was still snow under the trees and even snow on the path as we hiked higher. How good it seemed to me to be doing this with you, once again!

We talked a bit, remembered how scared we'd been, years ago, that we'd run into bears. That first year we were just kids and leaped with fright every time a chipmunk rustled in the woods. (Of course, when we got home we boasted like mad. How cold it was! How dark the night! How many animals crept up on us! How brave we were!)

By the time we got back from our hike, we were ready for supper. Again the usual, gathering wood, building a fire, cooking our meal, and sitting on logs to eat out of our tin camping plates. "Food never tastes as good as it does here," you said. You always say that. And I always say, "I'm three times as hungry here as I am at home!"

Then, just as we do every year, we sat in front of our fire while the darkness came down, and sang songs. That first year we sang out of sheer terror of the dark. Since then, it's become one of our traditions. I did notice that your voice was hoarse and not as strong as usual.

It became cold, very cold. We bundled up in jackets and hats, hid our hands inside our sleeves. The stars came out. An icy sparkling night. You sneezed repeatedly, and finally we got out our sleeping bags. I crawled in fully clothed, and so did you. We lay one on each side of the fire, and how still it was. How utterly quiet. I felt I could hear the stars shining in the sky.

It got colder still. I curled up in my bag, pulled my hat down over my ears. "This is the coldest night we've ever had," I said. "I'm sure of it."

"I th—th—think so," you said.

I thought you were making your teeth chatter on purpose, and I laughed. But, only a bit later, just as I was falling asleep, I heard you say, "Richie . . . are you awake? I'm freezing, I'm so cold—"

I still didn't realize you were sick. I mumbled something and dozed off again. The next thing I knew, you were shaking me. "Richie. *Richie* . . . Can't get warm . . ." You had your sleeping bag with you, but you crawled in with me like a child, shivering and chattering. "I'm so *cold*," you said forlornly. I hauled your sleeping bag over us for extra warmth. You kept shaking. I put my arms around you, held you tight, and finally we both fell asleep.

When I woke up, you were out already, building the fire, appearing perfectly normal. I sat up. "Steve? Are you all right?"

"A little woozy, but okay," you said.

But something was wrong. (No, not your health anymore. Whatever it was that hit you had come and gone.) You didn't look at me. You hardly spoke. It seemed all you wanted was to get back home. Couldn't wait to cut our trip short. Of course, you'd been sick the night before—but, all the same, I felt there was something more. . . . Those hours of being so close to me, Stevie, did they disgust you, finally? Is that it? You'd had enough of me, and too much, as it turned out.

On the trip back (which we took slow, for your sake), we had nothing to say to one another. We, who always have too much to talk about! What silence. Oh, how it hurt. All the way home, I talked to myself. *Look, Richie, it's utter nonsense to go on like this. How many times do you have to come to the same conclusion? It's hopeless, hopeless. . . .*

And that's how it happened that, just as we got home, as we were about to part, I said, in the most abrupt way, "Steve, I have to tell you something."

You turned. "Yes?"

"Steve—" I choked, forgot everything, then out it came. "I love you!"

The look you gave me! Was that horror I saw on your face? Is it so disgusting to you that I love you? Am I so repugnant? Such an animal? I'm struggling not to hate you, Stevie, for the silence and the look that greeted my words.

Oh! How unfair—I'm crying . . . crying over you . . . I must have made you up, invented my wonderful Stephan. If you were everything I thought, wouldn't you have said *something*? Wouldn't you have known the pain I was in, despite the idiotic way I acted? Wouldn't you have said a few words, at least, to help me out? Patted my hand, or given my arm a squeeze? Anything! Any little token to show you were human, and that you have a heart that can feel for other people!

As it was, you gave me this murderous look, stood tongue-tied for what seemed like hours (I suppose it wasn't more than a minute) and then bolted across the hedge to your house, dropping your sleeping bag along the way.

Oh, what an ending to our weekend—No, to everything. To our friendship, first—and after that, to my love for you. Because I assure you, Stephan, I will do my utmost from this moment on to cure myself.

It's done, Stevie. And I dread tomorrow morning. I dread it with all my heart, because, much as it hurt when I loved you secretly, it hurts even more to know that I've finally cut you off. That there's no more hope.

Good-bye, Stevie.

Dear Steve,

How many times have I started letters to you and said, *This is the last letter*? Well, this *is* the last. The final. The one letter I may (or then again, may not) send you. This letter is to say—Steve, how could you? How did you? It was you, wasn't it? Or is it possible that I've misunderstood?

To begin with—this morning I avoided you, and easily, since you were avoiding me as well. I went off to school—maybe I should say slunk off. I moped along, trying not to think of you, but going over and over in my mind that moment when I blurted the truth to you. What I said, how you looked, how I felt, what you did, et cetera. And each time I went over it, I felt more miserable, berated myself more harshly.

Why wasn't I content to let things go on as they were? What possessed me? Why did I have to change everything? Ruin what we had—our friendship! And now, having made it impossible for us to ever again be at ease with each other in the old way, I felt utterly bleak, forlorn, friendless, and even weak. It seemed an effort just to put one foot before the other.

A car passed. "Richie!" Jasper and Lucille. I grinned and waved and stepped along, unwilling to let anyone know how I was feeling.

"Want a ride?" Jasper called.

More grins and waves, and then they were gone, bombing out of sight under the railroad overpass. And

I moved along, numb inside, went all the way to the end of Branden Street, then turned and ran back to the overpass.

I'd seen it, Stevie, seen what you'd done, but seen it without seeing. The words didn't register. The change didn't penetrate that fog in my mind.

But at the end of Branden Street, I suddenly realized and ran back, telling myself all the way, Richie, you're hallucinating. Don't get your hopes up!

So then I stood under the overpass and looked up where, so many times before, I'd seen the scrawl, AVIE LOVES RIC FOREVER. It seems it's always been there, spray-painted on the bridge. And it was still there, the same purple Day-Glo, but a little changed. Three letters added. Only three. So that now it reads, STAVIE LOVES RICH FOREVER.

Stavie? You, Stevie? Rich? *Me?*

Stevie. Stephan. Steve! Is it some awful joke intended to make me suffer even more? I can't believe it. It's not your character. You're not mean and small. But, then— is it the truth? Does it mean that you— Is it even you, who— *Later.* Dear Steve, dear Stevie, *Stavie*—dear, dear, darling Stavie! You've just left, we've talked for hours, and yet it's not enough for me. Now I know everything. Now I understand. Yes, it was *you.* I could hardly believe it when you told me how you hung head down over the bridge and added those letters. You, Stevie! And scared every moment. But determined to do it. To tell me in a way that would be unmistakable.

You've told me everything once, then twice, and yet I long to hear it all again. How *it* happened to you the night you were sick. Yes, exactly what happened to me in your sister's kitchen. You *knew*. There, in the sleeping bag, you knew. You knew that you loved me, and you felt it was hopeless. I had never shown (you said) the least sign of considering you anything but a friend, and one that I took utterly for granted.

Stevie, I still don't believe all this. Do real stories end this way? But it's not an ending, is it? For us, Stevie, it's only the beginning—everything starts now for us. Our whole lives begin. Good night, Stevie, good night, but never again good-bye.
Your Richie.

Do You Really Think It's Fair?

Well, here I am.

What? I'm Sara Gorelick! Didn't you ask me to come to your office? Mrs. Teassle *said*— Oh. No, I guess we haven't met before. But I know who *you* are. So, what's up?

You've heard about me? I didn't know I was famous. The *famous* Sara Gorelick! . . . What?

No, I don't want to be a movie star! A model? *No.* Well . . . a judge.

Uh-huh. You heard me right. A judge. I don't think that's so funny. What's the hilarious joke? Yes, you are too laughing at me! I know when somebody is laughing and— Look, *you* asked me to come down here. You *asked* me. That means I don't have to stay, doesn't it? I can leave, right? Because if you asked me to come to your office just to laugh at me—!

Sensitive? I'm not *sensitive*. No, that's *not* the way I would describe myself. I'm—I'm—I'm *tough*. Okay? Now would you *please* tell me why I'm here? Which one of my teachers complained about me? Bet it was Sweetie Sorenson. It was, wasn't it? Just because I told him that assignment was dumb.

Yes, I did say that. Interview somebody who's over thirty. What does *that* mean? What's so gorgeous great about being over thirty?

It *wasn't* Mr. Sorenson who—? Oh, it was, but— *what*?

A consensus of my teachers? Yes, I know what that means.

Where? Where does it say that about me? Has become unruly and— Why can't I see the rest of that? Privileged material? That's just another way of saying you don't want me to see it. Why do grown-ups lie to kids? Yes, they do. All the time. Sure, I can prove it.

They lied in the hospital. They said Jayne would come out of it. Would live. They said it. Two doctors— An honest mistake?

Oh, it's always a mistake when you're grown up. If you're a kid, it's murder, right? If a kid had been driving that car . . .

You know what the judge said? He said it could have happened to anyone. That's a lie. He said it wasn't the driver's fault. No charges. Because the sun was in his eyes, and Jayne ran out into the street. That's all lies. He didn't say anything about the man drinking. And Jayne *didn't run out*. She looked both ways. Eight years old—she's not *dumb*.

She *looked*, and that man, that driver—we shouted at him. All of us. We saw it. We saw Jayne running out after the ball. We saw the car coming and coming, and we all started shouting and screaming. Stop! Stop! Stop!

No, I'm not crying. *No*. I am *not* crying. I don't cry. What?

Because I don't want to, that's why! Why should I cry?

You want me to cry? What business is it of yours if I— What are you, weird?

Yes, sure, McClure, that's a *good example* of the way I talk to everyone!

Yes, I know why I'm here. You want to brainwash me. Make me be polite and nice and good. Good little girl. Make goo-goo eyes at people. Or maybe you'd just like to put a piece of tape across my mouth! Look, I'm going now. I don't want to stay here. There's no law says I have to stay, is there? Swell, Mr. Fell! *Good*-bye!

You wanted to see me again? So what's new, Mr. Blue? Do you remember my name this time? Sara, without an *H*. Oh, I'm feelin' just fine, Mr. Cline, how about you?

Stop spinning around and sit down?

Okay, I'm down. Well, what's it all about? Here I am, and let's get it over with.

What?

I don't have much to say about it, do I? I mean, you asked me, but I *have* to come, don't I? Anyway, I don't care. I'm cool, Mr. Ghoul. I get out of Music this way.

Sure, I can guess why you asked me to come back. That report—unruly Sara Garlic!

Garlic? Joke. Family joke.

How do I feel about my family? Fine.

How do I feel about school? Blaaagh!

How do I feel about *you*? You really want to know? Or you want me to lie? You want me to lie, don't you? Nobody asks a question like that and wants the truth.

You do?

Uh, okay, you asked for it. How I feel about you— uh, nothing special. You know, shrug. Yawn. Blah, blah, blah, that's your job, isn't it? Talk, talk, talk. You want me to leave now? You want to put me in a corner? You want to send me to detention?

What? I can say *anything*, and it's okay? You won't take it personally? What if I mean it personally?

You still won't take it personally.

Uh, great. What are you, nuts? I mean, that is *really* weird. Koo. Koo.

Why you asked me to come here? That's easy. To braid my brains. To mangle my mind. To . . .

No, I don't think you're a shrink. You're a guidance counselor. A psychologist, right? What word? Psychologist? What's the big deal about knowing— What? The difference between a psychologist and a psychiatrist? One has to be a doctor. You didn't go to medical school, did you?

What? Well, I read a lot. Everyone in my family reads a lot—my mother, my father, my sis—

We all like to read, okay! Is that such a big *D* deal?

What was I going to say about my sister? Nothing!

No, I was *not*, I didn't even mention her name. Forget it! I don't want to talk about her.

What? That's one of the tasks you and I— I don't get this. What do you mean, a *task*?

Yes, I know what a *task* is.

Talking about my sister is a task? Is why I'm here? Then maybe I just better leave. Because I'm not going to talk about her. No, I'm not. And I'm not going to cry, either. You have got some very mixed-up, crazy ideas. I thought you got me here because I'm giving my teachers trouble and . . .

No, I don't think there's anything wrong with crying. If that's what you want to do, be my guest. I'll bring you a box of Kleenex. Just, *I* don't want to. Can you understand that? You dig, Mr. Fig? Don't want to cry. Do not want to cry. No cry. Sara no want water to come from her eye. Is clear?

Clear as water? Very funny, ha ha. Dr. I. C. Brains has big sense of humor. Can I go now?

What?

No, oh, no. Oh, no, oh, no, it-doesn't-have-anything-to-do-with-Jayne! I told you. I AM NOT GOING TO TALK ABOUT HER.

Yes, I'll talk about my family. I don't see what difference it makes to you, though. My dad's an electrician, my mom's a PN. Okay? Enough?

Yes, my mom likes working, don't you?

Uh-huh, Community Hospital on Greene Street. Right, same street we live on, but the other end, way down. No, she mostly rides her bike there. My father needs the car.

What?

Yes, that's my whole family. My father, my mother, and me.

You can't see my face? That's because I'm not looking at you.

Because I *feel* like sitting this way. Does a person have to sit a special way in your office? Next time I'll wear my T-shirt with Wonder Woman on the back so you can look at *her*. No, I'm not getting upset! Do you want to ask me anything else, or can I go back to my class now?

No, there's nothing I want to talk about!

I just told you. I'M NOT UPSET. I'M FINE. I'm mellow, Mr. Bellow. All right, all right, I'll come back. Next week, yes, okay. Next week.

*   *   *

Sara Sass reporting in, sir!

Nice shirt you're wearing. Do you always sit that same exact way? With your fingers together? Maybe I should sit behind the desk and you could sit right here in the hot seat. You need a little head shrinking? A bit of brain unkinking? Sara will save you. Is that a smile I see, or a frown?

Oh—neither. Do you think I'm being fresh? Rude? Obnoxious? Unruly?

Won't answer, will you? I can say anything, right? But that doesn't mean *you* stop thinking, does it? Bet you think I'm a weird fresh brat! That's why I'm down here. Right? Freshness and general messing up. General Messing Up reporting to Sergeant Scrambler. Were you in the army, Private? Is that why it says on your door—

What?

Am I going to settle d—

I thought you *wanted* me to talk. Just trying to please, talking up a breeze. Last time you were practically *begging* me—

Do I know— *Yes*, I know what *appropriate* means.

Gotta get down to business, huh? Oh, right, right, must get on with our tasks. Where's the mop and pail? Or do you want me to wash the windows? Or should I clean your desk, that's a *mess*, wow, my mother wouldn't stand for—

What?

You don't think we're going to get anything done this time if I—

Well, I don't care, Mr. Hair. It doesn't matter. You're the one who keeps asking me to come here. Am I driving you up a wall? That's what Mrs. Clendon said to me. Sara, you're driving me up a wall! Oh. You know about that. Were you shocked? Were you surprised? Were you real mad?

Well, because you're supposed to be working miracles on me, aren't you? Making me behave. Be a good little Sara.

No, I don't dislike Mrs. Clendon. She's pretty nice for a teacher. Then why do I— I don't know. Just some devil or something gets in me, I guess.

I know.

I *know* that.

I know I was never a troublemaker. Well, there's always a first time, ha ha. Who cares anyway? It doesn't matter.

Why do I keep saying *what*? That it doesn't matter? Must be because it's true. It doesn't matter.

What doesn't matter?

Nothing.

Nothing matters. Everything is all crazy and weird. The *world* is weird. You know? It really is. That's what I think. The world is weird and unfair. It just really *stinks*.

Sure, I think that. *Sure*, I do!

No, those are not tears in my eyes! I wish you wouldn't keep saying that! How many times do I have to tell you the same thing? I do not *cry*, mister. I-do-not-cry. I do *not* cry. I do not, I do not, I do not!

Hello.

No, I don't mind that the office is dark. I like to be someplace dark when it's raining outside.

What?

Quiet? I can be quiet, too. I'm not a freak, you know. I'm not just a big loudmouth.

You never said— But isn't that what you were thinking?

No? Well—if you say so.

Sure, we can talk. What do you want to say?

Yes, I have friends.

Best friend? Callie Gerstein, I guess.

Naturally I talk to her. Was she—? Yes, she was there the day Jayne— A whole bunch of us from the street. We were playing softball and— Do I have to tell you that all over again?

Did Jayne have friends? Yes, *sure*. Well, I had to watch her, that's why she was with—

Look. Is this some kind of test or something?

Well, the way you're asking things. They did that to Jayne once. Sneaked a test on her when she was in first grade. Asked her a million questions and then wanted to skip her to third.

No. My mother wouldn't let them. Was I— Yes, I was glad. That would have put her practically in my grade. Who wants their bratty little sister—

Sure, she was a brat! A big brat! And she always

had to hang around with me. Drag! Double drag! *Because* my mother *works*. Somebody has to look after— I mean, somebody *had* to— Why are you asking me all these dumb questions?

What? *Yes*, I know what ground rules are.

Yes, I'm listening. I don't have to look into your big baby blues every *second* to listen.

I *know* you're just trying to do your job— All right, all right, I'll *try*. But if *your* ground rule is for me to answer the questions, *my* ground rule is for you to stop asking if I know what every other word means! Yes, you *do*. What am I angry about? Nothing! Who says I'm mad? I don't care what you say it sounds like, *I'm not mad about anything*. I want another ground rule! You don't tell me what I am! Like angry, or unruly, or—

Yes, I'll answer your questions, I *said* I would. I keep my word. Do you?

Okay! It's a deal, Mr. Seal. Go ahead. Shoot. Ask me anything. . . . Jayne? Tell you about Jayne? Do we have to—

Okay, okay, I know. You ask, I answer.

Jayne. She was my sister. That's all.

A memory? Any memory? Just start anywhere? I don't know where to— I told you, she was a brat, a real pest, a baby who bugged me. Made me crazy sometimes. Like how? Like when I got a bike for my birthday. I was nine. Thought I was so grown up. They gave me a two-wheeler. Right, Jayne was four. She had a trike of her own. But she had to learn to ride *my* two-wheeler, or *nothing*. She must have fallen a million times. Skinned her knees, bloodied up her hands. Almost knocked out a tooth.

Everybody told her, *Quit*, you're too little.

She didn't quit. She learned to ride. The seat was too high for her. She didn't care, she stood up on the pedals. *No*, I wasn't *proud* of her. What for? After that I had to share my bike with her. Every time *I* wanted to ride, *she'd* be on it. My mother would say, Share and share alike.

No, they didn't. Said she was too young. Said bikes were too expensive. Said when she got older, and more careful.

I don't know. Maybe next year they would have.

What? It was a *Raleigh*. She messed it up. Full of scratches. Dents. She banged it up a million times. Never used the kick stand, just let the bike drop on the ground. She never took care of anything. In our room— Yes, same room. We live in an apartment—two bedrooms. I keep begging my parents, Let me sleep in the hall! My mother says, Nothing doing.

Why do I want to— Because Jayne is such a slob. Never picks up her clothes or books or— Can we talk about something else? Is the time up yet? I'm—I'm sort of tired . . . don't want to talk anymore.

Wednesday? All right. Ten o'clock? Keen, jelly bean. I'll be here.

* * *

Here I am again.

Yes, I'm ready. Yes, I remember our ground rules. Do you? You've got more to remember than I do.

What?

Go through my *anger*? I told you I'm not—

You want me to understand *what*?

The *steps* of sorrow? Ah, ha ha. Where do they lead to? Is it just one flight? Can I run up them, or do I have to walk slowly, like a lady? That's what Mrs. Christmas told me yesterday. Sara Gorelick, ladies don't run, they *walk*. What'd I do? I laughed. What would you do if someone— Oh, it's no good asking you, anyway, guys never get told stuff like that. Lester Coleman, gentlemen don't run, they *walk*. Can you hear it?

We're getting off the subject?

Oh, right, right, back to the steps of sorrow. Take 'em two at a time, gang.

Look! There's no rule that I can't make jokes. Lots of things are jokes. Oh, I forgot, you like tears better than laughing, right?

I'm being recalcitrant? Wow-ee, that's a mouthful. Uh, uh, uh, can't ask if I know what it means! Ha! But—I'll tell you this. If you were my dad, instead of that you would have said, Sara, you're acting like a regular little *jackass*. Ha, guessed it right, didn't I?

Sure, I'm in good spirits today. The sun is shining and I ate my Rice Krispies this morning. Yippee. Only pretty soon, if I have to go on listening to this lecture about the three steps of sorrow, I might feel like throwing up my snap, crackle, and pop.

Hey. Did I make you feel bad?

I didn't mean anything. Just joking around.

Oh. You're just thinking of where to start this morning. Whew. Had me fooled for a minute there. I thought the talking question machine was running down. No such luck, huh?

Tell you about Jayne? Again?

All right, *again!*

What did she look like. Skinny, sort of dirty blond hair, freckles. Right, right, we don't look anything alike. She's like my mom, I'm like my dad. Pretty? I don't know. Cute, I guess. My mom would send me to the store for milk and bread. And Jayne would say, Can I come with you, Sara? Can I come with you, Sara? Just to shut her up, I'd say, Okay! She talked so much. Just like you. Blah, blah, blah, she never ran out of stuff to talk about. You think *I* have a big mouth . . .

People would look at her and say, Your little sister is adorable. Those freckles! And they'd smile and pat her on the head. She was real jumpy about her head being patted. One time a man in the supermarket said, Hello, little girl. And he goes to her head, *pat pat pat.* It really set her off. Leave my head *alone*, she yelled.

She just couldn't stand the feeling of being bonked

on the head. Nobody ever asked her. They just figured, She's a kid, so that gives them the right to smack her on the head.

Yes, I think adults run the world. Don't you? Kids don't have anything to say about anything . . .

Maybe we *could* do a better job. Maybe we'd be a whole lot more *fair*. What do I mean by that? Can't you figure it out? Give you an example? Sure! That man who ran into Jayne. What happened to *him*? He didn't even have his license taken away. And he was drinking. Drunk. Yes, he *was*. I smelled it on him. He got out of his big car. Big black Chrysler. Jayne was lying there in the road, and I smelled it on him. I smelled it on him!

What?

Yes, I know. I know they said it wasn't his fault. But they didn't even say about him drinking when he went to court. Do you think that's fair? Yes, I was there. We all were. Me, Mom, and Dad. We heard the judge. We heard everything. They didn't ask me, no. Because I'm just a kid, maybe. Or maybe because of who he is, his name—

What's that got to do with—?

Are you *kidding*? His name is the same as Senator— What? He's his *brother*. That's right, his brother, and he should be in jail. I would have put him in jail. When I'm a judge, I won't care who anybody is. I won't care if the *President*'s brother comes in my court. I'll just listen to the facts and I'll make everybody tell the truth!

There's the bell. Good-bye!

Hi.

No, I don't feel like sitting down today.

There's no place to walk here. How come your office is so small? It looks like they made it out of a closet. They *did*. This really used to be a closet? Tacky!

So what's your question today?

Do I dream about Jayne?

Boy, you know how to pick 'em. I bet you put in lots of time thinking up these questions. Am I going to ans— Okay, okay. Answer: I don't know. Maybe. Sometimes. I don't want to talk about that.

All right! I'll keep my promise! What do you want to know? A dream I had about her? Okay, I dreamed we were on a horse together. Satisfied?

You're not.

All . . . right. I'll tell you more. A big white horse. And we were galloping across a field. . . . I don't know what kind of field! Does it matter? A field, just a field, ordinary, with flowers and bees and things.

I don't *know* why I dreamed that. You just dream things. No, we never had a horse. Jayne wanted one, though. She was horse-crazy. Her side of the room was all covered with horse pictures. Once, when she was about six, she begged Mom and Dad to get her a

53

horse. My mother said even if we could afford it, which we couldn't, where would we put it?

And Jayne says, In the backyard.

What a dodo. Our backyard is just about big enough for the clothesline.

So, next, Jayne says, I'll keep him in the bedroom. I'll get a pony and he can go at the foot of my bed.

We were all laughing. Zowie! Did that make Jayne mad. Her eyes are sort of greenish, and when she gets mad, they go all dark, and then her face gets bunchy and red, looks like her freckles are going to jump right off her skin.

My mother says, Someday your face is going to freeze like that, Jayne, and then you're going to be one strange-looking kid. And Jayne goes, Ha! Ha! Very funny! Boy, that's really funny! And then my father gets into the act. Don't be fresh to your mother.

And Jayne goes Ha! Ha! again, right in his face. Which is big dumbness. You can say lots of stuff to my mother. But my father—no. So he gets mad and gives her a whup on the behind.

No, she didn't cry. You couldn't make that kid cry. Not that way. She'd cry if she found a dead animal. One time she found a mouse that a cat killed. It was stiff, with blood on its neck. Jayne picks it right up and puts her hands around it, like she's going to warm it up and make it live again.

I go, Come on, Jayne, it's dead. Put it down. It's full of germs.

And she goes, Listen, Sara, *listen.* I can feel its *heart.* And she wants to bring it home and take care of it. Yeah, she did it. Sneaked it into the house and kept it for two days until it started to stink and my mom found it.

Sometimes I could persuade her to do things, but mostly, no. Nobody could. She's just stubborn. Like the time Mom cut my hair. Wanted to cut Jayne's hair, too. Oh, no, you don't, Jayne says. Oh, no, you don't.

And she's backing away, holding her hair like Mom was going to chop it off right to the roots. So Mom and I both try telling her how cute she'll look.

She says, Who cares! I want my hair!

Then we say stuff like how much easier it will be to comb and all that. And Jayne says, I love my hair!

And she runs into the bathroom and locks the door and won't come out until Mom promises, sacred word of honor, not to cut her hair.

My father says we all let her get her own way too much. I sure agree with him! That brat can be stub born, and *dumb,* too.

Like *what?*

Like once she jumped into a lake from a second-story window. Because somebody dared her. My mom said she could have been ki— Is that dumb enough for you? Can we change the subject now?

Games? Sure we played games together. Just dumb kid stuff. You don't want to hear—

You do.

You are the most curious person I ever met. You are a real big *B* brain picker.

Games. Right.

Umm . . . one we played was lying on our beds and walking our legs up the wall to see who could go the highest. Jayne always won, because she would walk herself up until only the back of her head was on the bed.

You want *more*? Whew. You're never satisfied. Okay, we played our-favorite-room—telling about this room we'd have if someone left us a million dollars and we could buy anything we wanted. Uh-huh, Jayne always puts a horse in her room. It's one of her favorite games. She goes, Can I go first, Sara? I have to go first, Sara! Sara, if you don't let me go first—! Bugs me *crazy*.

What? *What?*

There's some *confusion* in me—? I don't know what you're talking about.

I *what?* . . . Sometimes I talk as if Jayne is still alive? I don't know what you mean. I'm just telling you things. You ask, I tell. Like I said, Keen, jelly bean.

Why are you so picky anyway? What if I do talk about her as if—

Yes, I hear you. I'm *listening*. I understand. I'm not stupid! You think I don't want to face facts.

No, *I* didn't say I don't want to face facts. I said that's what *you*— Oh, what's the use? Forget it!

No, I AM NOT GETTING MAD. AND I AM NOT GETTING UPSET. Do you have to keep ASKING me that?

Are you kidding? Mad because Jayne died. Mad at *Jayne*? That would be super dumbness, wouldn't it?

If you want to know if I'm mad at anybody, it's you, Mr. *B* Brain Picker. Yes, *you* make me mad. You make me see red, white, and blue! How mad do you make me? THIS mad! THIS mad! THIS MAD THIS MAD THIS MAD THIS MAD!

What? Did it feel good banging my fists on your desk? Why should it feel good? I hurt my knuckles. My throat is sore. *No*, it's all *right*. Leave me alone. Can I go now? You don't want to talk to me anymore, do you?

That's true, Mr. Rue. I don't want to talk to *you* anymore. How much of this do you think I can stand? Nothing personal. You said I should say what I felt, honestly. So I'm saying it. GOOD-BYE! And If I never see you again it'll be too soon for me!

Heigh ho, Mr. Snow.

You mad at me?

I didn't think so.

I'm right on time today.

Yes, it's a beautiful day. Uh-huh, very warm. No, I don't mind sitting down. Here on the windowsill okay? I *like* it better, is why. If you turn around . . . see, no big desk between ` `. More *equal*—

Why did I use that word? What word? *Equal*? I don't know. Just said, More equal.

What does it remind me of? Oh, boy, picking my brains again.

Oh, okay, I'll humor you. One and one *equals* two. More? Great.

Are-you-*equal*-to-the-task-we-are-all-created-*equal*-in-the-eyes-of-God. What's this all about, anyway?

Am *I* equal to the task of saying Jayne is de—

Why should I say that? What *difference* does it make? I know she's—I *know* what happened—

I *told* you . . . I can say it if I *want* to!

I-just-don't-want-to.

What? You want me to say it anyway? Just to prove— Big deal! My sister is . . .

Why do you want me to say it?

No, I am *not* afraid to say it! MY SISTER IS DEAD. There! Are you satisfied now? God! *I hate you.* No, don't touch me! Leave me alone! *Leave me alone.* I'm going now. I'm going!

Hello?

Should I, ah, come in?

Hi. . . .

I'm quieter than usual? No, I'm not. I'm like this lots of times. I just haven't got anything special to say.

I've been feeling—okay. . . . Sure . . . okay . . . What?

Do I realize . . . *ten minutes*? I haven't said anything for ten minutes? Just been sitting here?

Daydreaming, I guess.

No, nothing special. Just about something that happened once. You probably don't want to hear. I mean, you're more morbid. You like to tune in on funerals and accidents and . . .

Now I sound more like myself? Old Sassy Sara? How come you smile when you say that?

Oh. Uh. Well, I like you, too. But don't go getting a big swelled head about it. You're not the only grown-up in the entire world that I like, you know!

And I don't even like you that much, anyway.

Oh, back to *that*.

It was something that happened on Halloween. The Parks Department had a fair. You wouldn't be interest— You would be. Okay, if you *insist*.

Well, there was this fair, like I said. And I wanted to go, and Mom said I had to take Jayne. I didn't like that. Callie and I wanted to go alone. We already took Jayne out trick-or-treating. She was seven—it was last year. She says, Oh, please take me, Sara! I'll be good! I promise. I'll give you my stuffed kangaroo.

Big deal. Just what I wanted, her stuffed kangaroo that she still chewed on when she sulked.

Yes, I took her. I had to. There was this huge crowd in the park. Booths selling popcorn and candy apples, and a beauty contest booth, and this one place where you went in, got a slimy trickle down your back, and then a skeleton jumped out at you. We went in there. It was crazy. We were screaming and laughing. We did some more stuff, but all Jayne wanted was to go over to the greased pole. I had to yell at her every two minutes to stick with me and Callie.

Then one time I turned around and she was gone. The greased pole, naturally. Because they promised anybody who climbed to the top a pony. Free.

Uh-huh, they greased the flagpole in the middle of the park.

Oh, sure, you could get your legs around the pole, and start climbing, but not far. You'd slide right down, 'cause you couldn't get a grip with your hands. And meanwhile you get covered from head to toe with grease!

But that's where Jayne was. No, not watching. *Climbing.* She'd go up and she'd slide down. And she'd go up again. I yelled at her to come down. She didn't even look at me. Just kept trying. And this humongous bunch of people are watching her. Jayne, come down, I yelled again. And she yells back, Sara, I got to climb this pole!

And she's wriggling up like a monkey. And sliding down.

She just kept trying. And trying. I don't know how long. A *long* time.

People were clapping for her, saying stuff like, Go, Freckles! Way to go, kid! Stuff like that.

You wouldn't believe what she looked like when I finally dragged her home. Jeans, shirt, face, hair, arms—everything, *total* grease.

You dumb kid, I said. I'm yanking her along by the

hand. Why didn't you come down when I called you? Wait till Mom sees you!

And she goes, I could've climbed that pole if you didn't make me come down, Sara!

Make her! I go, You are stupid. Nobody could climb that pole. Why do you think they said they'd give a free pony?

Shut up, she goes. Sara, you're an ass! Then she sort of jumps on me, gets me all greasy, too, and pounds on me and yells, Shut up, Sara! Shut up, Sara! Keeps saying that. Shut up, Sara! Shut up, Sara!

Then we get home and my *mother* yells at me. I told you to watch her, Sara! I thought I could depend on you! I thought you had sense!

She got Jayne cleaned up and we went to bed. After a while Jayne goes, Sara?

And I go, Don't talk to me!

And she goes, My feet are cold. Can I get in bed with you? And before I can say anything, she's out of her bed and in my bed, pushing me over and strangling me with her arms around my neck. Her hair still stinks of grease. So I shove her away. But I can't shove her off me. So we fall asleep that way, and— and—

What?

I am not crying. Don't look at me!

No, I don't need tissues. Keep your stupid tissues! Why did you get me talking about— Oh, *no.*

All right, I'm *crying.* Are you happy now? You

made me— Just leave me . . . *just leave me* . . .
Jayne . . . she left me . . . oh no, no, no, no . . . no
. . . noooo . . .

Hi. You ready for me?

The last session? After this you don't think I have to
come back unless I feel like talking? I always feel
like talking. But not to you, ha ha.

Oh. You're still being serious. Right. Question. Shoot.

How did I feel after I cried? Do you have to be so
personal?

All right, I'll answer your question one more time!
I didn't like it. No, I didn't like crying!

You're smart. Can't you guess why? Don't you *know*?
If you cry, you could cry everything away. Everything,
everything.

What do I *mean*?

I mean what I say. Everything I remember. Everything I feel. If I cry it all away, won't I forget? Yes,
and then—and then Jayne will really be gone, won't
she? That's my question for *you*.

Yes. Yes, yes, I know. You've said it to me. It's a
fact. She's dead, I know— See, I can say it if I want
to. She-is-dead. My-sister-is-dead. And I cried. You
should be very happy. That's what you wanted.

No, there's no more I want to say.

Uh-huh, I guess it's good that I talked about her. If
you say so. And cried. Yes. I can see your point. Yes,
I'm sure you're right. I'll feel better now, yes.

Only . . .

What? I was going to say something else? Oh.

Oh, just one thing.

I can't stop thinking one thing. Do you think it's fair? That Jayne is dead? Do you really think it's fair?

De Angel and De Bow Wow

At night, as a small girl lying in her narrow bed, rain or snow streaking the window, Bibi heard her mother and her mother's best friend, Zenetta of the big red arms, talking in the kitchen. She heard the clink of their cups, her mother's deep voice, and Zenetta's loud laugh. Outside she heard dogs barking and the ambulance screaming up to the hospital; and in the apartment next door the neighbors singing; and in the little dark front room her grandfather, a thin old man who wore high-top shoes all year round, talking back to the TV. "*Basta!* Don't know what your face is saying!"

Zenetta worked in the Christopher Bakery and always brought a bag of day-old rolls and bread. She had a husband and twin girls and knew everything going on everywhere on Greene Street. It was Zenetta who told them that Ed Wixner, the shoe repairman, went into the hospital for appendix and found out he had cancer. Zenetta who told them every time Mrs. Lillian's smart lawyer daughter came to visit. And Zenetta who knew first who was getting married, who was dying, and who was going crazy behind the walls of their house.

Even before Bibi knew Celia or Jimmy, Zenetta brought their names into her mother's kitchen. Celia was "that gorgeous little Vronsky girl, never says a word. You ever see such big blue eyes?" As for Jimmy DeAngelo and his mother, it seemed to Bibi that Zenetta knew everything there was to know about them. Not only because (according to Zenetta) Mrs. DeAngelo talked constantly about her beautiful Jimmy, but also because they lived in a little run-down place right next door to the Christopher Bakery. Mrs. De-Angelo, Zenetta reported, liked this house because it had a driveway where she could park her white Caddy. Almost everyone else with cars on Greene Street had to park in the road. Mrs. DeAngelo also liked this house because it was cheap rent.

Mrs. DeAngelo worked in Autolite and made good money, but, Zenetta said, preferred putting it on Jimmy's back instead of into the pocket of a fat landlord. "That boy is the best-dressed kid around. Nothing but fifty-dollar sweaters for him. You know she's got another one, older boy, out in San Diego? She don't care two piffles about him. Not one red cent does that one get out of her."

"Doesn't seem right, a mother not loving her kids the same," Bibi's mother said.

"Doesn't," Zenetta agreed. "Now, me, I can't choose between the twins. Sometimes can't even tell the difference between them. *He*"—this was the way she referred to her husband at all times—"can't *ever* tell the difference." But talking about her own family was never as agreeable to Zenetta as talking about others. She went back to the DeAngelos. "That older boy, he cleared out so soon as he was sixteen. Whoosh! He was gone."

In her bedroom Bibi heard her mother sigh. "Life ain't easy."

"Yeah," Zenetta answered, "but it's all we got." And then the two of them laughed together in such a jolly manner that Bibi knew that what she wished for more than anything in the world, more even than a doctor kit or a Barbie doll, was also to have a best friend.

In kindergarten she met Celia Vronsky when they were put next to each other in the Listening Circle because of their names. First came Andrew, then Bibi. Next Celia, then David, and so on. That was the way Bibi learned her alphabet—Andrew Bibi Celia David, but then the Listening Circle jumped to Frankie, and she always did have to stop a moment and put the *E* in there between the *D* and the *F*.

Every day for the first week they were in kindergarten, Celia cried her heart out. Just sat in her chair in the Listening Circle or stood next to the big red blocks or near the door, crying. One day Miss Loden said, "Celia Vronsky, if you don't stop crying, I'm going to put you in the cloakroom and close the door." Celia cried harder. Bibi, who didn't like the dark cloakroom, said, "Miss Loden, don't you do that!"

Miss Loden had black hair in a big puff on top of her head. "Bibi Paladino, you'll be next if you talk to me like that."

Miss Loden didn't scare Bibi, but she thought if Celia had to go in the cloakroom she'd never, ever stop crying. She whispered, "If Miss Loden puts you in the cloakroom, I'll go in, too." And she squeezed Celia's damp hand. After that she was the only one who could get Celia to stop crying.

Everything about the two girls was different. Sometimes, as they got older, Bibi said, "You and me make just one perfect person." Because she had all the nerve and Celia had all the looks: a delicate blond girl with eyes like blue fish. She was so beautiful that Bibi often wanted to put her arm around her friend out of sheer admiration and joy, but Celia would stiffen and look frightened. "I don't like to be touched," she explained once.

"We're sure vice and versa," Bibi said. She loved hugging and jumping around and kissing. Her grandfather was always calling to her mother, "Marie, stop this skinny little devil." In the morning Bibi would grab the old man and kiss him and nuzzle his neck.

"Oooh, Grandpa, I like the way you smell." And evenings, if her mother wasn't too tired, she'd sit down in the front room with the TV on and Bibi would sit in her lap. Even when she got to be a pretty big girl, Bibi would still sit in her mother's lap to watch TV.

Bibi and Celia played all the usual games—jacks, potsy, king-of-the-hill, red rover, and their own private games, too. They'd play What-do-you-wish-for-most-in-the-world? Celia would say, "I want to live someplace quiet and nice, have *my own house*, and people have to *knock* on the door to get in."

Bibi would say, "I want to go places, and see everything, and have all the money, and buy clothes and furniture and all the stuff I want."

When they were nine years old, they made a pact. "Let's never get married, Bibi," Celia said.

"It's okay with me."

"You gotta swear."

"I swear," Bibi said.

"You swear on your life?"

"I swear on my life."

"You won't ever forget?" Celia said.

Bibi shook her head.

"Say it," Celia said.

"I won't ever forget." Later, when she was a little older and dreamed about getting married in a long white gown, she didn't want to tell Celia.

"Were you a beautiful bride?" Bibi asked her mother.

"Sure," Marie said, "and your father was as handsome as a movie star." Their wedding picture was right on top of the TV in a gold-leaf frame. "I wish you knew your father, honey," Marie said. "He was a sweet, sweet boy."

Bibi's mother almost got married once more. She met Red when he came to fix the drying machines in the WE-R-FAST CLEANERS where Marie worked. Red told her jokes and funny stories, took her to the movies and once to dinner at The Clamshell. The next week he came to dinner at their house. He called Bibi "Bibi Biscuits" and gave her fifty cents. Pretty soon he was coming to eat with them almost every night.

"Geez," Bibi told Celia, "he's got red hair and freckles all over. I bet he's even got red hair on his butt."

"You're crazy, Bibi," Celia said, and she laughed so hard she got the hiccups.

Bibi liked Red's jokes and how much he made her mother laugh. But after a while some of his jokes didn't seem that funny. He'd come in, wipe his feet on the kitchen mat, look at Bibi, shake his head a long time, and say, "Now, who's this ugly kid? What's she doing here?" Once, in a low voice, he said, "You're creepy-looking." Bibi couldn't be sure if she really heard him say that, because the next moment, in a honey voice, he said, "Supper ready, Marie?"

"Not yet, Red."

"Okay, I'll go clean up." Every night Red went into the bathroom, stayed there for maybe an hour. Grandpa's bladder wasn't so good, he had to pee a lot, and he'd hang around the bathroom door, knocking now and then. "You going to stay in there all night?" A while later, another knock. "Somebody else here needs to use the place."

"Hang on to your pants, old man!"

Right then Bibi's mother would bang down a pot lid or slam a cupboard door. She'd be in the kitchen fixing something good to eat, wearing her old yellow sneakers with the toes poking through. As soon as Red came out, she'd say, "You think that's a nice way to talk to an old man?"

"He bugs me," Red whined.

"That's my father, and you're gonna respect him. Don't forget, this is my house."

"You tell the bum, Marie," Bibi's grandfather yelled from the bathroom.

One night at the table Red started talking about what a funny-looking kid Bibi was, just kept talking like that, not noticing how Bibi's mother and grandfather were giving him evil looks. "Marie, you're a big, good-looking woman. How'd you ever get a skinny, ugly kid like this Bibi?" The grandfather slapped him on the side of the head. Red yelled. Bibi's mother yelled louder. After that Red didn't come back.

"Good riddance to bad rubbish," Bibi's mother said to Zenetta.

And Celia told Bibi, "You're lucky he's gone. You don't want to have a stepfather. Like me."

"Why not?" Bibi said. But that was all Celia would say about it. But Red had been right about one thing.

Bibi *was* skinny, and there was nothing pretty or pleasing about her pinched-up little penny of a face, the eyes set too close, the nose too big. Sometimes, in school, the boys made elephant noises when they passed her. And once, in the cafeteria, a whole tableful of boys had gagged at sight of her.

"How come I'm not pretty?" she asked her mother.

"Who cares about pretty?" Marie said. "You got spirit. You got something better than pretty." And she spit out of the side of her mouth to show Bibi what she thought about *pretty*.

"Celia's pretty," Bibi said. "She's beautiful."

"Celia's always crying," her mother said.

"Not so much, anymore," Bibi said loyally. The older Celia got, the prettier she'd become. In the streets people were always looking at her and smiling. Teachers made her their favorite, and boys didn't leave her alone. But Celia would bite her fingers and say, "They don't know me, Bibi. You're the only one I love. The only one I can talk to."

Bibi and Celia agreed they didn't care about that pretty/homely stuff. They just liked being together.

The fall they were both eleven, the Parks Department put on a Halloween Fair in Greene Street playground. There were booths, prizes, games, and races. The first thing they saw was a banner: SIGN HERE FOR BEAUTY CONTEST. "Celia, you gotta enter," Bibi said.

"Oh, no, I couldn't." And Celia started biting her fingers.

"You gotta, 'cause you would win."

"Oh, no, no, don't say it, Bibi."

"Maybe you'd win five dollars," Bibi argued. But when she saw how upset Celia was, she relented. "Never mind, we'll do something else." And to make Celia laugh, she said, "I'll go skin up the greased pole."

Just then a boy ran into Bibi and thumped her hard on the back. "Clumsy turkey, David Kowalski," Bibi yelled after him. "I'll knock your block off." Then another boy ran by her, looked at her, and barked. More boys ran by, laughing and barking at her. "Bow wow! Bow wow!"

Celia found the piece of paper stuck on Bibi's back. I'M A DOG. BARK IF YOU AGREE. Celia's face got red and she started to rip the paper.

"Hey, gimme that," Bibi said. Her belly felt as if she'd just eaten a piece of her grandfather's stinky cheese. She stuck the sign square on her chest.

"What're you *doing*?" Celia said.

"It's *my* sign," Bibi said, and she spit out of the corner of her mouth.

Celia's lips wobbled. "You're crazy."

"Yeah, I guess I am, just crazy old Bibi," Bibi agreed, and she wore the sign the whole time they were at the fair. I'M A DOG. BARK IF YOU AGREE.

One of the boys that had barked at her was Jimmy DeAngelo, who lived down the street with his mother, next to the Christopher Bakery. Half the girls in school were in love with Jimmy, a boy with long-lashed dark eyes and good manners. Girls clustered around him in school and hung around outside his house, looking around and laughing a lot. Celia and Bibi talked about Jimmy, too. "Do you think he's conceited?" "Do you think he's stuck-up?"

They had a secret name for Jimmy—De Angel. Bibi said to Celia, "You and De Angel have to get together."

"Oh, no, not me," Celia cried.

Then they'd play a game, man and woman, and take turns being De Angel. When it was Celia's turn to be De Angel, she'd touch her fingers to Bibi's and say, "Oh, Bibi, I adore you, do you want to marry me?"

Bibi, on cue, would answer, "Jimmy De Angel, I promised my best friend I would never get married." Celia would then be caught between a frown in her role as De Angel and a smile, as herself, at Bibi's answer. And Bibi couldn't resist adding, "But, my lovely De Angel, we can still have fun together." When it was her turn to be De Angel, she'd put her arms around Celia, but very lightly, very carefully, so as not to make her nervous, and say, "Oh, Celia, you are so beautiful and I am so handsome, we are like two movie stars, ain't it true we make the perfect couple?"

Celia's answer never varied. "Jimmy De Angel, I don't care to get married to any man!"

By now Bibi knew that Celia's stepfather, whom her mother finally kicked out, used to bother Celia. Bibi was the only person who knew this. Celia had sworn her to silence. They had taken a blood oath: jabbed needles into their fingers and mixed their blood.

All through junior high and into high school they

remained best friends. Sometimes, after they'd talked on the phone for an hour or two, Marie would say, "I don't know what you'd do without Celia, Bibi."

The summer they were sixteen, Celia and Bibi worked at K mart and saved their money, going to the bank to deposit together every Friday. They agreed that as soon as they had enough money they'd take a trip to either Mexico or Alaska, whichever one Bibi decided on. Then they'd save some more money and buy a house and live in it together. Celia's mother had married again, and although her new stepfather was okay, Celia still thought about having her own place. "Promise you'll come live with me, Bibi."

"I don't hafta promise. Who else would have me?" Bibi laughed. She always laughed when she said things like that. At sixteen Celia was more beautiful than she'd ever been, while Bibi was just as skinny and just as plain. *Ugly* was her secret word for herself, but she couldn't say that around her mother or Celia without their yelling at her.

Every day that summer they took the bus downtown to work, and every night they took it home. Bibi studied maps and Celia, biting a pencil, checked out the real-estate ads and furniture sales. Neither one spent money on anything, aside from a few movies. They planned to continue working when school started, and agreed that if anyone wanted to give them birthday presents, from now on it should be money to add to their trip and house fund.

Then, right after the summer, the week before

school started, Celia's family moved to Alaska, where Ted, her stepfather, had a new job on the pipeline. Nobody had even told Celia they were going to move. "They're leaving right away and I *have* to go with them." Celia was crying so hard, nothing Bibi said could stop her. Three days later she was gone.

It was as if someone had suddenly stuck Bibi in a box. Cut off her air. Locked her in. There was a pain in her chest. She wanted to drop out of school, but Marie asked her to stick it out for a while. "You'll make another friend," Marie said.

It rained all through September. Rained all through October. The newspaper said it was the wettest September and October in history. In November it turned cold. Bibi didn't care about the weather. She had stopped crying, went back and forth to school, and worked weekends at K mart. But the pain in her chest was still there.

One morning, when she got out of bed, she looked out the window and saw the telephone lines sagging with ice. Up and down Greene Street, cars were coated with ice, tree limbs had snapped, and the sidewalk was as sleek and smooth as a skating rink. Bibi wondered if this was what Alaska was like. Everything was closed down—schools, shops, and stores. Her mother didn't go in to work; they all stayed in the kitchen, listening to the radio and eating fried tomatoes and eggs.

Zenetta came over later, sat down at the table, folded her big red arms, and said, "Did you hear? Did you hear about poor Mrs. DeAngelo? I found her." Despite the storm, Zenetta had been on her way to work. Inching along the slick sidewalk, she had almost passed the DeAngelos' little house when she saw something lying in the driveway next to the white Caddy. "At first, I thought it was a dog, something like that. Wasn't even gonna stop, it was so slippery." When she investigated, she found Mrs. DeAngelo, half under the car, still wearing her robe and slippers, her head cracked open. The ambulance came, but even though the hospital was just down the street, it was too late. "I bet she went outside to check on her car," Zenetta said. "Make sure the storm hadn't damaged it. Slipped on the ice, and that was *it*." Zenetta snapped her fingers.

The service for Mrs. DeAngelo at Meekham's Funeral Home was crowded with kids who had graduated with Jimmy the previous year and with neighbors. Jimmy's older brother, a skinny man wearing glasses and a frown, had flown in from California.

All through the service Jimmy cried. Afterward everyone went up to him and said something. When Bibi's turn came, she said, "Geez, Jimmy, I'm sorry for your loss," and she squeezed his hand. He looked at her with wet black eyes. *What* a face, she thought, a little ashamed to be so frivolous on such a sad occasion. To make up for it, she squeezed his hand harder and said, "Don't you worry, Jimmy, you got lots of friends."

"Thanks, Bibi," he said, "but nobody could be a friend like my mother." And again his eyes filled. It just about broke Bibi's heart, the same way she used to feel when Celia's eyes blurred with tears.

A few days later, passing Jimmy's house on the way home from school, Bibi thought, If Celia was here we'd go right in and cheer up Jimmy, tell him some jokes or things. She'd heard Zenetta talking to her mother, saying how Jimmy hadn't set foot outside his house since the funeral. "I wonder what will become of the poor boy," Zenetta said. "How can he get along on his own? You know, his mother did everything for him."

Bibi kept walking, but now that she'd started thinking about Jimmy she couldn't stop. Felt sorry for him and, well, something else, too. Wasn't she the only one who could ever stop Celia from crying? Cheer her up? Make her laugh? Bibi had a funny thought, then. God made some people like Jimmy and Celia— so beautiful you didn't want to stop looking at them. And then He made some people like her—monkey-faces. Maybe it was all for a good reason—like the monkeyfaces had to be matched up with the angel-faces.

The next day she walked right up the narrow walk to the DeAngelos' front door and knocked, loud and cheerful. After a couple of minutes Jimmy opened the door. At first Bibi was scared he didn't recognize her. Then he said, "Oh, Bibi. Hello." He looked bad, stains on his shirt and his beard growing in, in patches.

"Hey, can I do anything to help you out?" Bibi said.

"What?" Jimmy was smoking and he had a dazed look.

Bibi glanced past him into the house. What a mess.

Clothes all over—she saw a pair of dirty socks right on the table—crusty dishes on the windowsill and the floor, dustballs everywhere, and the whole house didn't smell too good.

"Hey, Jimmy," she said, "your mother didn't keep house like this, I bet. Let me help you clean up a little." She walked right in, almost laughing when she thought that Celia always did say she had all the nerve.

Jimmy sank down into a chair and stared as Bibi started picking up stuff. She piled dishes in the sink, dumped cigarette butts into the garbage, swept the floor, and opened a window to air out the place. "How about picking up your clothes, Jimmy?" she said. "Put them in the hamper or something." He nodded and got up. "What'd you eat today?" she asked. Except for sour milk and a piece of moldy salami, the refrigerator was empty. In the cupboard Bibi found a can of clam chowder, heated it, and cooked a pot of noodles.

"Come on, sit down." She poured the soup into a bowl and set the buttered noodles in front of Jimmy. "Dig in," she said, sitting down opposite him. "You gotta eat, Jimmy." Her tone was frank and friendly, just the way she'd always talked to Celia. Jimmy just sat there, looking like he was a war victim.

"I guess you miss her a lot," Bibi said.

"You want to know something? The morning she went out—to check the car? She left me a glass of fresh orange juice. Not the frozen kind, she never used that. She squeezed it fresh for me, every morning, before she did anything else."

"She took good care of you," Bibi said.

"She understood me," he said. "It wasn't just the orange juice. She always understood me. And now I'm so ashamed." His eyes watered.

"Hey," Bibi said, "you got nothing to be ashamed of, Jimmy. You were a good son."

"No," he said. "I never told her how much I loved her."

A couple of days later Bibi went over again, cleaned up things, and cooked Jimmy a meal. She got into the habit of dropping in after school, cooking supper, then sitting around talking to Jimmy about his mother and work. Just before his mother died, Jimmy had been laid off his job in Highgate Motor Sales. "They said I was one of the best salesmen they ever had, Bibi."

"I believe that, Jimmy."

"But they had to lay off someone, and I was low man on the totem pole."

"You'll get another job, Jimmy."

"That was a good job, wish I had that one again."

"Maybe they'll call you back. I bet they will!"

Sometimes they played cards or watched TV. One thing Jimmy especially liked was when Bibi read the newspaper to him while he ate supper. His mother used to do that. They'd laugh over Ann Landers, check out the letters to the editor, and talk about which movies were playing.

Jimmy was looking better, shaved, and wearing clean jeans and one of his V-necked wool sweaters when Bibi came over. Sometimes she ate supper with him. He always asked her, but usually she refused, because her mother expected her for supper, too. All day in school Bibi would plan what she was going to cook for Jimmy and think about the things they'd talk about. It made the dull hours pass and helped her forget how much she still missed Celia.

Bibi was a good cook. She'd been standing at Marie's elbow in the kitchen since she was a little girl. Jimmy went crazy over the way she cooked chicken with pineapple juice and tarragon. "Not to be disrespectful to my mother," he said one day, "but you beat her at cooking, hands down."

"Hey, I gotta do something good to make up for this mug," Bibi said.

"Looks don't matter," he said, and he gave her a hug.

"They don't matter if you got 'em," she said with a big laugh. Jimmy still had his arm around her waist. "Jimmy, you remember when those kids put that sign on me at the Halloween Fair? 'I'm a dog, bark if you agree.'"

"I don't remember that," Jimmy said.

"Well, I do," Bibi said.

That night she wrote Celia a letter. "Ain't life funny? You in Alaska, and me friends with De Angel. If you were here, it would be perfect."

A few days later, when she walked into Jimmy's

house, she found him lying on the couch, feeling bad. "I got to thinking about my mother." Bibi patted his face and his head. "Jimmy, you're gonna be okay. Listen, Jimmy, she's in Heaven now." She made him get up and wash his face, while she cooked supper for him. She'd brought a pint of his favorite French vanilla ice cream.

Later, it came out that he was blue for another reason, too. No money. The rent was due. The Caddy people were coming to take away the car. He'd already missed two payments.

"Do you think your brother would help you?"

"He doesn't care if he never sees me again. Lucky he came for my mother's funeral. I need a job, Bibi." For a couple weeks now, Jimmy had been looking for work.

"No luck today?" Bibi said. "Where'd you go?"

"McPharry's, that furniture place on the boulevard."

"You'd be some good furniture salesman, Jimmy."

"I wouldn't mind selling furniture at all."

"Maybe I can help you out," Bibi said. "I got money saved from the summer—"

"I couldn't take your money."

"Sure, you could. It's just sitting in the bank. You can pay me back when you get a job."

"Bibi, you're the best," Jimmy said, and he got up and hugged her and told her she was the only person left who cared about him. And before you know it, he was kissing her.

Geez! Bibi thought, I'm in heaven! And remembering how she and Celia used to play kissing De Angel, she couldn't help laughing.

"What's so funny?" Jimmy said. "Don't you like the way I kiss?"

Bibi could see he was getting upset. "I got a fault of always laughing at the wrong time," she said. "The way you kiss, it's heaven."

Then they kissed some more, and when they stopped to get their breath, Jimmy said, "Bibi, let's get married. I want to get married to you. You're the nicest girl I know."

Bibi couldn't even speak, just nodded okay. And they kissed again on the cheeks and on the mouth, and they were hugging and kissing so hard they lost their balance and fell down on the floor. And then they were both laughing something awful, and Bibi knew she'd never been so happy.

Going home, she was still in a daze. Me and Jimmy De Angel! But at home, when she looked in her mirror, she got sober fast. No, oh, no, this couldn't be De Angel's future wife. She didn't feel sorry for herself, just saw that she was what she was. Loved De Angel too much to think of him marrying Bibi Bow Wow.

She went there the next day as usual, cleaned up, and cooked a Spanish omelet and Pillsbury biscuits, and happened to notice one thing about Jimmy's manners. He used his biscuit to wipe up his plate. "When should we get married?" he said.

Bibi had planned all day what to say. "Jimmy, you don't have to do that. I release you," she said, a bit grandly. (She had heard that on TV.)

"You don't want to?" he said, his fork freezing in the air.

"Just because you said it yesterday, I ain't going to hold you to it, Jimmy."

"You don't want to?" he said again.

"Oh, I want to."

"Well, so do I," he said.

Her mother didn't want to give permission. She said Bibi should wait until she was eighteen. "You don't want to have a baby so young, honey."

"I'll wait for the baby," Bibi said. And she thought how pretty Jimmy's babies would be.

"Well, does he love you?" Marie said.

"Hey, you think no one could love this face?"

"Now, I didn't say that, Bibi!"

They were still going at it when Zenetta came in, put her big red arms down on the table, and said, "Bibi, you know I love you like a mother, so don't take me wrong, but Jimmy DeAngelo could have any girl in the world. So, why you?"

"Why Bibi?" Marie slapped her hand on the table. "Because the boy loves her, that's why. Bibi, you want the wedding right here in our house?"

After that, Jimmy brought over his clothes and his mother's double bed and this and that, and they moved everything into Bibi's room. It was December then, and they went to church one Saturday afternoon and got married. Her mother cried, but Jimmy winked at Bibi and she wanted to laugh, even though it was a solemn occasion. She had a new yellow dress and a bouquet of tea roses. Mrs. Lillian was there, Zenetta, the neighbors who always sang—almost all the same people who had gone to Mrs. DeAngelo's funeral. Her grandfather's legs were feeling weak, so he didn't come, but when they got home, he gave Bibi ten silver dollars and said, "You're a good girl, Bibi. I wish you all the luck."

In January, Bibi quit school and took her job in K mart full time. Marie didn't want her to do that, but Bibi couldn't see freeloading off her mother. Every week she gave her mother room and board money, took some for herself, and gave Jimmy the rest so he'd feel good. He hadn't found a job yet.

Celia wrote her a letter. "I still can't believe I'm looking at your wedding picture. I guess we were silly kids—remember our vows and stuff? Maybe I'll go to college. I haven't made up my mind."

Every morning Bibi and her mother ate breakfast together and left for work together, and every night they came home about the same time and made supper, taking turns with the cooking, now that Bibi was a real married woman. Then, when everything was ready, they'd call Jimmy and Grandpa and they'd all sit down together. Jimmy smiled at Marie, asked about work, and said how good the food was. Marie wouldn't want to smile back, Bibi could see that, but she nearly always did. After supper the two women did the dishes and ironed and folded clothes while, in the front room, Jimmy talked to the grandfather.

And later, in their bedroom, he and Bibi would tell each other everything they'd done that day. For Bibi, that was the best part of every day except sometimes, in the morning, when she'd wake up, look at Jimmy sleeping next to her, and think, This is Jimmy De Angel, he's my real husband now.

Zenetta came over to visit, brought a bag of sweet rolls. "How's the old married lady?" Some girls from school came into K mart. "Geez, Bibi, never thought you'd get married so soon. Isn't it something, you being married to Jimmy DeAngelo."

"Being married is great," Bibi said, flashing her wedding ring. "You oughta try it."

But there were little problems. Hard to find enough time to do everything. Sometimes she got real tired. And Jimmy was still out of work. He missed having a car, too. They talked it over, decided to save money for a down payment on a car—not a Caddy. One of the economy cars, maybe a K Car. They saved their money in a Paul deLima coffee can. They liked to count it together, see how close they were coming to having the down payment. Jimmy studied the auto magazines so they'd be sure to get the best buy.

"Well," Marie said one night when she and Bibi were doing the dishes, "it's nice having a man around the house. I admit it. And Jimmy's a nice boy, even Zenetta admits he's settled down."

Things were going good, and then it seemed as if

they got to the top of a hill and just naturally had to slide down. Bibi wasn't surprised. All along she'd been waiting for that slide. Jimmy picked up an ear infection, he was sick for a couple weeks, and the doctor bills were awful. No money went into the Paul deLima can. Jimmy was cranky all the time he was sick and, even when he got better, didn't get into a good mood. He didn't want to talk, watch TV, or even go out and have a beer. Sometimes he'd lie on the bed, hands behind his head, staring at the ceiling, and not saying anything for hours. It spooked Bibi.

"You two fighting already?" Marie said.

"No fights," Bibi said. That was true. Jimmy didn't like fighting, he was never nasty or mean, just said, "Leave me alone." Bibi wished he *would* fight. She knew more about that than "Leave me alone."

It was February, and instead of snow they had rain every day; the whole city was gray, and mildew got into the bathroom and on the kitchen walls. Jimmy hated the weather and stayed in all day.

One night Bibi and Marie were scrubbing the bathroom. "You think your husband is going to get a job?" Marie said.

"Yeah, he will," Bibi said. "He's had tough luck."

"Luck's not going to get any better if he just lies around reading dirty magazines all day."

"Leave him alone," Bibi said.

"I don't touch him. I'm just reporting what Grandpa says."

"Grandpa is an old man." Bibi wrung out a rag.

"Don't be disrespectful. Jimmy's not looking for a job. He's letting you work, period. He's found himself a soft berth, my girl. That's what I'm afraid of."

Bibi bent over the tub, scrubbing at one spot. "He's still feeling bad from his ear infection." Her heart pounded, she was scrubbing so hard. That spot wouldn't come out. She scrubbed harder.

"You're making excuses for that boy."

"I don't want to hear no more!" She flung down the rag and went to her room. Jimmy was lying on the bed, reading a magazine. She stood at the foot of the bed. "Hello." Jimmy didn't say anything, just lay there in his green flannel pj bottom, showing his smooth chest, looking handsome and sad.

Bibi held up the new pink nightie she'd bought on her lunch hour. So pretty she couldn't resist it. "Like my new nightie?" She shook his arm. "Jimmy!"

"How much did it cost?"

"Me to know, you to guess."

"Ten bucks." She shook her head. "Twenty?"

"Getting close."

"More?" He pushed himself up against the pillow. "Now we won't have anything to put in the coffee can again."

"Well, I wanted something pretty. I work all week and I wanted something pretty for myself." And then, unable to resist, she added, "You want to put money in the coffee can, get a job."

He flushed. "So you wanted something pretty. Is that it?"

"Yeah," she said, recognizing the challenge, "want to make something of it?" And she didn't even care that she'd given him that dig about a job, because fighting at least made him talk.

"You wanted something pretty?" he said again. And he smiled, showing his teeth.

"What's so funny?" Bibi said. "Must be really funny to get a smile out of you."

"Yeah, it's funny." He pointed to the nightgown, then to her and said, "Bibi Bow Wow." He said something else, too. But Bibi didn't hear the something else. She went right into a daze, just like the day he asked her to marry him, couldn't speak, and fell back against the pillow. Didn't say anything. Not a word. Hardly breathed.

"Bibi?" he said. "Say hey, what's the matter, Bibi?" Still couldn't speak. "Hey, *Bibi.*" A look in his eyes now, as if he was scared. "It was just a joke," he said. He closed his hand around her arm. "It was just something to say. You're not taking it serious, are you?"

And still Bibi couldn't speak. Oh, the pain she felt, something pressing behind her ribs, the worst, most awful pain she'd ever felt, worse even than when Celia left her. She raised her hand, opened her mouth to speak, let her hand drop. And a tear fell from one eye.

"Hey, hey, hey." Jimmy bent over her. "Bibi, hey! Hey, Bibi, I *love* you."

Then she looked at him, her beautiful husband, her Jimmy De Angel with the long lashes. "I love you, too," she said, and she kissed him on the shoulder.

91

And then, right where she kissed him, she bit him, bit so hard she broke his skin.

He yelped. Little drops of blood came up in a half circle from her teeth marks. "You bit me," he said. He touched the blood. "You bit me." He sounded so surprised, so hurt. "Why'd you do that?"

"I don't know," Bibi said. "I guess I'm just crazy." And, right then, she remembered how her mother would say to Zenetta, "Life ain't easy," and how Zenetta would say back, "Yeah, but it's all we got." And how they'd both laugh, so jolly and sad at the same time.

"I don't know," she said again. "Life ain't easy." And she put her face up against Jimmy's and laughed and laughed. And, after just a little bit, he got to laughing with her, too.

Summer Girls, Love Boys

The summer she was fifteen, Mary Lewisham (but not in this order) cut her hair, met Bobby Nicholes, and, in a booth in the second-floor lav of the public library, read a lipstick-scrawled injunction: *Summer girls, love boys!*

"Oh," Mary wrote underneath, in a handwriting not quite bold, "I want to."

Mary's birthday was early in July. Her parents took her out for dinner at their favorite restaurant, the China Doll Inn. They liked the name of the restaurant, they liked the food, and they liked walking from their home on Linden Avenue over to that part of Greene Street that was a little run-down (but still okay), where the restaurant was snuggled between a shambling old house and a bicycle repair shop. Mary's present was a handmade Kabuki doll for her doll collection, now numbering thirty-nine, and all presents from her parents. Everything Mary owned came from her parents. She, herself, had come to them late in life; and they often told her how long they had waited for her, how fervently they had wished for her, how much they had adored her from the instant of conception.

"So now she's fifteen and probably thinks that's the whole enchilada," Mary's father said, as they ate their won ton soup. "Probably, she'll just get too big for her boots now, Mommy."

"Poppy, you're terrible. Isn't he terrible, Mary?" Her mother lightly slapped her father's hand. In their family playfulness, Mary and her mother were always allied against her father—the two women bravely sticking together.

Mary's father had a small kindly head set on an enormous bloated body. He was an insurance agent and had once been featured in "Business News of the Week" in the morning newspaper. Her mother, small and round, was "proud to be a housewife." Her hands, rarely still, were knobby from arthritis, while Mary's father's hands, often lying composed in his lap, were plump and soft.

"Probably now that she's fifteen, she'll turn into a juvenile delinquent," Mary's father went on, "and torment our old age with her shenanigans." Her father often teased Mary by talking about her as if she weren't present. He would say slighting things about her character or her appearance because, as her mother had told her, he actually thought Mary was perfect.

Mary always laughed at her father's teasing, although even when she was small it had faintly humiliated her. To be talked about as if she had no ears, no eyes, no existence in the here-and-now gave rise to odd, ghostlike feelings. And lately Mary often did have strange thoughts. Did she exist? And if so, who was she? To her parents she was certainly someone: their Mary Frances, their only child, born to delight them.

After Mary's birthday celebration, the long, hot days passed slowly. Mary took a piano lesson once a week, swam in the Greene Street School pool, and sometimes baby-sat for the two Fellman kids. And then, too, she spent hours dreaming, wishing she weren't fifteen. It seemed to her awful to be fifteen, neither child nor adult.

"Summer girls, love boys," Mary whispered to herself. There were moments when she sizzled inside, as if she were made not of bones and blood, but a mass of sparking, snapping wires. Moments when she thought she could not bear another instant of the summer to pass in the same, slow, hot, unchanging way.

Mornings, lying in bed, gazing at the shelves of dolls on one wall (United Nations dolls, antique dolls, Shirley Temple and Barbie and Diana Ross dolls), the faces of people she knew, and bits of conversation, and odd phrases passed through Mary's mind.

It came to her one morning, as she looked at the

dolls in their sparkling costumes, that she *hated* their simpering faces, their stiff arms and legs, and their perfect glossy heads. She sat up with the surprising thought and said into the dimness of the room, "I've *never* liked dolls."

Another morning, an entire incident from years ago came back to her. She and three girl friends had decided they had to see the breasts on a new girl in school, humble and detestable Ava Schmith. They were ten then, a raunchy, dangerous age. They laid their plans—to capture Ava, to carry her off to the cellar of a deserted house, to pull off her blouse and look. Mary was the one who said, "We have to have flashlights."

But on the day of the abduction she stayed home from school with a "sore throat." "I was sick," she told her friends the next day.

"You missed something," they said, and they poked each other and smirked in a way that made her unsure if they had gone through with the abduction or were just tormenting her for not having shown up. For having been "sick."

"Oh," she cried. "Oh!" As if it were all happening again. She felt with a kind of sick shame the flatness of her life, that she had always been too careful, too good. And one of those odd things she kept on thinking popped into her mind: *How to break the enchantment of their love.*

It was that day she first thought about cutting her hair. Long, straight, and glossy, it hung below her

waist. Every Saturday morning her mother gave Mary
an egg shampoo in the kitchen sink, and often said
proudly, "Mary's hair has never been cut."

At lunch, poking at her cheese sandwich, Mary said,
"How do you think I'd look with my hair cut?"

"Cut your hair?" her mother said with so much shock
that Mary retreated and said, "Bangs. I was thinking
of bangs."

"Bangs?" Her mother studied Mary. Slowly a mis-
chievous smile appeared. "I guess Poppy would be
surprised, all right."

After lunch, with her mother watching, Mary cut
careful bangs straight across her forehead. "Oh, my,"
her mother breathed. "Oh, my. It's so different. I guess
it's beautiful, but I hardly know you! Look at your
eyes, Mary. Your eyes!"

Staring at herself in the mirror, Mary saw that she
did, indeed, look different, her eyes larger, her whole
face somehow transformed, as if by those few scissors
strokes she had been turned into someone else. Someone older, someone more mysterious.

"I don't recognize myself," she shouted gleefully.

"Mary, the *neighbors*," her mother said, standing
behind her, and they both giggled as they looked at
the new Mary in the mirror.

The next day, on her way to baby-sit for Jeanne and
Ted Fellman, Mary saw Bobby Nicholes sitting astride
his motorcycle on the corner of South Avenue and
Hurley Street, waiting for the light to change. She
knew him from school. He was older, a senior, a tall

handsome boy with thick, straight blond hair. He glanced at her, a casual dismissing glance, then looked again. "Hi," he said, taking off his helmet.

She thought of the graffiti in the library, the instruction (or was it an order?)—*Summer girls, love boys!*—and swung the red plastic bag in which she had a box of crayons and molasses cookies for Jeanne and Ted. "Hi," she said.

"You go to Jeff High, don't you? I've seen you around. Let's see, uh, you're—"

"I'm Mary Lewisham."

"I'm Bobby Nicholes."

"I know."

"Where you going, Mary? Want a ride someplace?"

"Sure," she said, her heart pounding dangerously.

"Hop on. I guess you've been on a cycle before."

"My first time," she said to the back of his head.

"Is that right?" Bobby swung around and grinned. "Hold on, you're in for something great." He fastened his helmet and kicked off. As they turned the corner, the ground rose toward Mary at a sickening angle. Gripping the seat, she kept her eyes open. I might die, she thought coolly, and a wave of exhilaration, what could only be called *joy*, shot through her.

When Bobby left her off in front of the Fellmans', he said, "Well, how was that?"

"Very enjoyable." Mary's legs wavered, and she clutched the handlebars.

"Enjoyable, huh?" Bobby laughed. "You're cute."

A few days later, she and her mother were outside on the stoop when Bobby drove past on his cycle. He U-turned and pulled up. "Hi, Mary! Want to go for a ride?"

"Yes," she said, standing up.

Her mother pulled at Mary's jeans. "A motorcycle? Mary. A motorcycle?" And standing up, she whispered, "Who is this boy, Mary?"

"He goes to my school. Bobby Nicholes. His father's a professor. He's a friend," Mary said in a rapid whisper. "He's a very nice boy."

"I wish he didn't have a motorcycle."

Bobby, sitting astride the cycle, one booted foot on the curb, called politely, "Nice day, isn't it?"

"You see," Mary whispered. "He's *nice*."

"I don't know—"

"Please, Mom, *don't*."

"Don't *what*?" her mother said. "Mary—"

But Mary was already at the curb, climbing on behind Bobby and fastening the red and white helmet he handed her. She sat very straight, gripping the seat behind her.

"Hang on to me," Bobby called as they turned the corner.

Her arms wound around his waist, Mary felt she was flying as they darted in and out of traffic. Wind lashed her face, the pavement churned by beneath her feet, and a jubilant little cheer—or was it a jeer?—rang in her head. Ya! Ya! Ya!

The next time Bobby came for her they left the city, rode out to the suburbs, and buzzed around on the wasteland near a gravel pit. Afterward, sitting outside a diner at a little round concrete table, their striped helmets on the ground next to them, they ate hamburgers and french fries. The sun beat down, they sipped sodas and smiled at each other.

It was, Mary thought, just like a scene from a movie. In a moment Bobby would slip his hand over hers. *Mary. Bobby's voice cracked with emotion. I have something to say. . . . I'm sure you've guessed . . . Mary . . . Mary . . . I've never told anyone this before. I love you, Mary. Oh, please. Tell me! Do I have a chance?*

". . . and I really wanted to pick up a job at that camp," Bobby was saying. "I mean, seeing as how Corky was working there—it would have been perfect, but I got in too late. So here I am, stuck at home and working as a bag boy at the Big G—"

"Corky?" Mary said.

"That's what I call her. Her real name is Cornelia. It was either that or Corny. You'd like her, Mary. She's terrific, she's just—" Bobby shook his head at the impossibility of describing Corky. "Beautiful, and—I tell her, her one fault is, she doesn't love my cycle. Wants me to get a car."

"What does she—" Mary began, then made herself say bravely, "Corky—what does Corky do at the camp?"

"She's a counselor."

"That's wonderful," Mary said.

"Oh, she's one of the best. The woman who runs that camp goes ape over her."

Corky was in a rowboat with two little campers. Suddenly, one of the kids jumped up to look at something in the water. The boat rocked, then it tipped over! They were all in the water. Of course, Corky could swim and was a lifesaver, but when she fell into the water, she hit her head on the side of the boat. She was knocked unconscious. People on shore rescued the two little kids, but Corky's body wasn't even found until days later. In his awful grief Bobby turned to Mary. She put her cool hands on his brow and gave him a reason to go on living. . . .

When Bobby dropped Mary off in front of her house, her mother was sitting in a plastic chair, a book in her lap and knobby hands exposed to the heat of the sun. "Hello, Mrs. Lewisham," Bobby called, making a little salute.

Mary's mother gave Bobby a nice smile, but when Mary joined her, she said, "Honey, Poppy and I have talked this over, and we don't want you going on that motorcycle anymore."

Mary just looked at her mother.

"It's dangerous, honey," her mother said. "Your father is an insurance man. He knows the statistics. It's a very dangerous way to travel."

"I always wear the helmet," Mary said. "And Bobby is careful. He's such a good driver."

———

103

"Honey," her mother said, "we're only thinking of you. We don't want anything bad to happen to you." And she looked at Mary so pleadingly that Mary gave her promise she wouldn't ride the motorcycle again.

The next morning she woke up depressed. Would Bobby want to see her anymore? Even before she knew about Corky, she'd guessed that what he really liked was playing big brother. Powering around the city with her clutching his waist, taking corners fast, showing off his cool dangerous style.

Bobby, my mother says . . . Bobby, my parents had this talk and . . . I know you're here to take me out on the cycle, Bobby, but . . .

In the end she decided she couldn't wait for him to show up. She'd go to his house and get it over with. *Bobby, guess what! No more motorsickle for me.* Make a joke of it. But, later, walking down Mohawk Street, coming closer and closer to the moment when she would have to tell Bobby, the same shame she had experienced when she didn't help abduct Ava welled into her throat.

At Bobby's house a man wearing beat-up sneakers and a skimpy pair of cutoffs was mowing the lawn. "Hi. Looking for somebody?"

"Bobby Nicholes?" she said.

"Ole Bobby should be zooming in any sec now. You want to wait?" Mary nodded. "Who are you?" he asked, leaning on the lawn mower. It was the old-fashioned kind you had to push by hand.

"Mary Lewisham," she said.

"I'm Allan Nicholes." He held out his hand. "Bobby's father." Mr. Nicholes gave Mary a lingering handshake. The whole thing surprised her—the way Mr. Nicholes had introduced himself, the handshake, the frank interested way he was looking at her.

Just then she heard the whining roar of a motorcycle. "Here he is," Mr. Nicholes said. "The working man." Bobby parked his cycle in the driveway. "How was work?" his father said. "A drag?"

Bobby gave his father an unfriendly glance. "Nobody says *drag* anymore. Hi, Mary, what're you doing here? Come on in."

The Nicholes house looked as if a wind had blown through it, scattering papers and objects in every direction. There was hardly a bare surface to be seen. Mary knew Mr. Nicholes taught at the community college and his mother had a framing shop in the mall. Everything about the Nicholeses, Mary thought, was more fascinating than her own dull family.

She followed Bobby into the kitchen, where he collected a bowl of grapes, then up the stairs into his bedroom. "Mary, this is really neat, you coming over." He put a record on his stereo. "I wanted you to hear this. Know this song?" In his funny voice, Arlo Guthrie sang, "I don' wanna pickle. Just wanna ride my *mo-o-ter sickle!*"*

---

* THE MOTORCYCLE SONG by Arlo Guthrie. © Copyright 1967, 1968, 1969 by Appleseed Music Inc. All rights reserved. Used by permission.

Mary shook her head, startled. She'd never heard the song before, but hadn't she just thought of saying to Bobby, *No more motorsickle?*

"Sit down, Mary." He shoved clothes and magazines off the end of the bed.

"I have to tell you something first." She stood in the middle of the room. "I can't go on the motorcycle any-more. My parents—" Her face flushed. She couldn't go on. Why had she agreed? Agreed, agreed, agreed. She agreed to everything! Suddenly she realized that, on that long-ago day when she was supposed to have shown up to abduct Ava, she had told her mother. Or her mother had gotten it out of her. *Her mother had known.* The conviction swept over her. Had known and kept her home. But, her shame, instead of lessen-ing as she thought this, only deepened.

"Parents," Bobby was saying. "Don't they burn you, though?"

She stood straight, one hand at her throat. Her voice revealed nothing of the inner turmoil. No one, glancing casually at her, would have guessed her pain. That's life, she said, we simply have to be brave. But Bobby broke down. You're leaving me, you're going away? Mary! Oh, Mary!

"So I guess, so I guess we won't be seeing each other anymore," she said.

"Don't be nuts," Bobby said casually. Straddling a chair, he threw darts at a giant Hitler poster. "Watch this, Mary, I'm going to get Hitler in the right eye." He held up his hand, dart poised. "You come over and visit anytime you feel like it," he said, releasing the dart. It landed on Hitler's nose. "Shoot!"

"It was really close," Mary said. She picked up a framed picture of a girl astride a horse. "Is this Corky? She's beautiful."

"Told you," Bobby said.

Corky sat straight-backed on the horse, her chin raised. Corky had character, Mary thought. She'd be a wonderful counselor and all her campers would fall in love with her. Mary had fallen in love with her counselor the summer she was eleven and had gone to camp for two weeks.

"Do you think she'd mind me being here in your room?"

Bobby drew back his arm, squinting. "She knows all about you, Mary. We're practically engaged." This time the dart landed on Hitler's chin.

Mary retrieved the dart from Hitler. *Corky and I are like this, Mary, Bobby said, holding up intertwined fingers, but that doesn't mean I don't have room in my heart for you. You're actually my best friend. There are things about you—well, you're so understanding, for instance, so sympathetic. I know I can tell you anything. The truth is I haven't dared tell Corky about you. I'm afraid she just wouldn't understand. . . .*

"Besides, you're only fifteen," Bobby said.

"What?" Mary said.

"I mean—" Bobby grinned. "*Fifteen.* I wouldn't rob the cradle."

Mr. Nicholes, Bobby's father, was surely good-looking, Mary thought, frowning at the Hitler poster. She raised her arm, holding the dart between two fingers. Even better-looking than Bobby, when you got right down to it. The dart landed almost perfectly between Hitler's eyes.

Mary didn't go back to see Bobby for a week. When she did, Mr. Nicholes was there again, this time weeding the garden. He stopped what he was doing to talk to her. "Nice to see you, Mary. How about a Coke? It's a real dog day." He went into the house, and Mary sank down on the steps. Mr. Nicholes was different, not like a teacher and not like a father, either. He was most like another kid, but older, with good manners.

Mary's grandmother in New Mexico was sick. No one to care for her except Mary. All flights were booked! Fortunately, a small, privately piloted plane was available. By an incredible coincidence, when she boarded the plane, she found Mr. Nicholes on it. Well, he said, his face lighting up, this is a piece of good fortune!—

"Doing anything special this summer?" Mr. Nicholes sat down beside her on the steps. He handed her a frosty bottle. He had a strong, sweaty smell.

"Just my music and—no, nothing special."

Over the rugged Grand Tetons, the plane was suddenly engulfed by a storm, a swirling mass of ice and snow. The pilot was flying blind, and . . . crashed. Only Mary and Mr. Nicholes survived. Alone, in the vast frozen wilderness, with nothing but the few pitiful things they salvaged from the wreckage . . .

"*You* should do something special, Mary." Mr. Nicholes leaned against her. "It's summer! Vacation time! Va-*ca*-tion!" He made a sorrowful face. "All year, classrooms, paper work, now it's summer again and, guess what, Mary? I still can't get away from classrooms and paper work. Don't you feel sorry for me, Mary?"

After that day Mary always hoped Mr. Nicholes would be home when she went to Bobby's house. But when he was, she never knew what to say to him. With Bobby, though, she was bold, she danced around his room and sang the motorsickle song in a silly Arlo voice.

One hot day when she walked over, neither Mr. Nicholes nor Bobby was home. She sat on the steps for a while. Marigolds, like hot orange suns, bloomed near the house. Mary walked to the backyard where there were a lot of overgrown bushes and sat down under an enormous old lilac. The sun came dappled through the heart-shaped leaves, the insects sang their piercing song. How slowly time passed. How long the summer seemed. She was fifteen and nothing had changed. Would sixteen be better than fifteen? She yawned with dread. Perhaps they would still say to her, *Anyway, you're only sixteen.* Would she have to wait still longer, and longer, and *longer* for her life to begin?

Mary Lewisham, world-famous correspondent for the biggest newspaper in the United States, was on her way to Europe on an ocean liner. Mr. Nicholes hap-

*pened to be on the same ship. Mary Lewisham often
saw him standing at the ship's rail, gazing into the distance. She thought of speaking to him, but, of course,
respected his privacy. His eyes were deeply sad. Mid-
way across the ocean, a storm came up, hundred-foot
waves battered the ship, and the order came to
abandon ship. In the panic Mary Lewisham and Mr.
Nicholes were outstanding in their efforts to save
others. They were the last ones to leave the stricken
ship for a life raft, and—*

"Hi, there, girl." Mr. Nicholes stood over her, hands
on hips. "What are you doing hiding out here?"

She stood up hurriedly, brushing off bits of grass and
twigs. "It was so hot," she said breathlessly.

"It was so hot," he mimicked, smiling. "Come on in
the house." And then, casually putting an arm around
her shoulder as they walked toward the house, he said,
"You are a very, very pretty girl. Do you know that?"

Her throat clamped, she felt the same surge of danger and elation that had gripped her on Bobby's cycle.
(Oh, she might have been killed! Anything could have
happened! And, even so, she had kept her eyes open.)
In truth, Bobby hadn't done anything that reckless. Still
—how satisfying to remember those moments.

"What'll it be, Mary?" he said in the kitchen. "Coke
or orange juice?"

"Orange juice, please."

Mr. Nicholes poured juice into the blender, whipped
it into a creamy froth, and filled two tall glasses. He
added vodka to one glass, then held the bottle over the

other. "You?" he said, smiling. Mary stared, blushed, and shook her head.

Mr. Nicholes clinked his glass against hers. "Well, here's to cooler weather, Mary." He leaned against the cupboard and his shoulder touched hers.

Months later, mere shadows of their former selves, Mary and Mr. Nicholes were rescued. Reporters surrounded them. How did you survive such incredible deprivations? I, said Mr. Nicholes, could never have made it without Mary Lewisham. She was my comfort throughout. She was magnificent. She was—

"Tell me, Mary. What do you see in that son of mine? I can't talk very easily to the fellow."

"Bobby is very sweet," she said softly.

"Also very lucky," Mr. Nicholes said. "Don't you agree? He's got a very pretty girl friend—you know about Corky, Mary?—and another extremely pretty girl at his beck and call." Mr. Nicholes leaned toward her. "What are you thinking, Mary? What a mysterious expression!"

His face was now so close to hers she felt as odd as if she had been playing statues and had just been violently whirled. "Oh, Fifteen," Mr. Nicholes said, and with a sigh he kissed her. There was a sweet oily taste on his lips. Dazed, Mary thought of marigolds, their blazing centers.

The front door slammed and Mr. Nicholes moved away from her and opened the refrigerator. "Want a Coke now, Mary?"

He held out the wet bottle and, from habit, from long

years of training, she responded politely, "No, thank you." A shudder passed over her and she bolted from the kitchen. In the hall Bobby was taking off his helmet.

"Hi," he said. "Just come over? What's the matter? You look weird."

She gave him a stunned smile and, walking out, closed the screen door carefully behind her.

That night, Mary and her parents ate in the China Doll Inn. "Let's have egg roll and spareribs tonight," her father said. He and her mother discussed the meal. "Do you feel like egg roll tonight, Mary?" her mother asked.

And her father playfully said, "She looks like a little egg roll. But don't tell her I said that!"

Her mother laughed and tapped her father's hand. "Now, Poppy!"

It was as it always was. As it always had been. But how strange Mary felt. The light in the restaurant was queer, a kind of greenish light, as if they were all underwater. And Mary felt heavy, even weary, as if she had been swimming through murky water for a long time. If her mother knew what Mr. Nicholes had done, she would willingly beat him with her clubbed knuckles; she would, in Mary's defense, tear out his hair or scratch out his eyes. And what did *I* do in my defense? Mary thought. The question surprised her and made her heart pound anxiously.

"Are you going to finish your rice, Mary?"

"More tea, Mary? Wasn't that good, though!"

"Yes . . . yes . . ." Mary murmured. The air was so

thick and green, yes so very like water . . . and her arms felt so heavy . . .

She was swimming, stroking strongly, when a frog— quite an enormous ugly creature—swam up beside her. The frog had staring yellow eyes that looked at her boldly. Don't you recognize me, Mary? the frog said. Good heavens, it was Mr. Nicholes!

"Fortune cookies, fortune cookies," her mother said. "Is everybody listening? This is my favorite part of the meal." Fumbling a little, she broke open the crisp shell.

The frog followed Mary as she scrambled up on shore. Go away, she said. Scram! Vamoose! You are ugly. But the frog stuck with her, looking at her from yellow eyes. Suddenly he leaped at her. Mary was taken by surprise, but reacted fast, moving nimbly out of his way. The frog leaped for her again. Why, no, you don't, Mary said. And jumping into the air, she came down foursquare on top of the frog. Mary, Mary, the frog gurgled, help, Mary, you're squashing me! Mary . . . Mary . . . Ma . . . r . . . y . . .

"Read your fortune, darlin'," her father said, nudging Mary.

She unfolded the slip of paper. "Patience. In time the grass becomes milk."

"That's all right if you want milk," her father said. He and her mother laughed with pleasure at his joke.

And Mary, looking from one to the other, thought, So much sadness of things. So much sadness of things. She didn't know where the thought had come from, only that she ached for them: she loved them so, yet did not love them as she once had, and could not, and would not, not ever again. And ached for herself, too. To still be fifteen—oh! To still be fifteen!

At home she closed the door to her room and took up the scissors and, cropping mercilessly, cut her hair. Cut all the long, dark, silky strands till they lay in piles around her on the floor, and her face emerged, nothing now between her and the world but a ragged head of hair.

Carmella, Adelina, and Florry

Mary Beth Lichtow   Mr. Nalius
American History, 4th period   October 10

ASSIGNMENT: AN ORAL HISTORY NARRATIVE
                FROM THE PAST

COMMENT: My mother talked into our tape recorder about the time she worked in a factory. Then I typed up what she said. It was extremely interesting. Until I had this assignment, I never knew my mom had worked in a factory!

My other comment is that when I did research for my mother's Oral History Narrative from the Past, I was really surprised to find out that only 20% of workers in the United States belong to unions. We did a whole unit on unions, so it seems they're very important. But if 80% of workers don't belong to unions, *they* must be pretty important, too!

(P.S., Mr. Nalius, maybe we can do a unit on workers who aren't in unions? And if such terrible things still happen to them, as happened to my mother?)

ORAL HISTORY NARRATIVE FROM THE PAST:

My name is Zelda Sagan Lichtow. I guess that's the first thing you'd want to know. I'm married, I have three kids, Susan, Jeff, and Mary Beth, and I work outside our home as a paralegal for Joffrey and Bogardus, who are terrific lawyers and married to each other. I only mention that last bit because it points up the fantastic difference between *right now* and the time I'm going to tell you about, which is the year 1949. That year I was nineteen and had just finished my first year of college.

In those days you might, just might, meet a woman who was a lawyer (or a doctor or an engineer) now and then, but most of us went to college to become teachers or librarians or social workers. It's only occurred to me recently that I have a real interest in the law, which is one reason I'm working as a paralegal. To sort of test the water, find out if I want to go to law school. I don't want to get off the point of my story, but this is background that I think is reasonably important.

Another thing about those days is that if you had the smarts to go to college, and if you could get up the money, you generally *stayed* in college. Dropping out was pretty much unknown, and certainly dropping out and then going back the way a lot of kids do today. In general everything about those days was less flexible than it is now.

Anyway, that fall when I was supposed to go back to school, I instead went to work as a punch-press operator in a mica-insulating factory. Now, to explain how I happened to go from college student to factory worker when I was perfectly happy *being* a college student, I'll have to tell you something personal about a boy I met. Actually I don't see how I can tell this story *without* being personal. (Besides, the idea that history isn't personal is ridiculous. What else is history, except people?)

Okay, it was 1949. A few years after World War Two, and just before the Korean War, and *long* before the Vietnam War. A lot less money around than there is now. That's what I meant about staying in college—lots of people were just too poor to get there. We were on the better-off side of poor. My father and mother had both worked all their lives. I mean my mother had worked *outside* the home, as well as *inside*. They had both come from poor families and each had left school early to help *their* families. Well, you can see why they didn't want us kids to do that, and they did everything possible to see that we all finished high school and went to college.

I knew all this, but, no, I wasn't rebelling when I dropped out to work in the factory. It was just that

that summer, while I was working in Rader's Cut Rite Drugs, I met Eric. Yes, enter Eric! An older man! He was twenty-five, and I was, well, *dazzled* by him. Maybe you'll think this is funny, but I'd had only one real boyfriend up to then. My parents had been *very* strict with me while I was in high school and when I got to college, things weren't all that much different. Colleges back then looked at themselves as *in loco parentis*—taking the place of parents, and especially for girls.

I had to be in my dorm by ten every night and have my lights out by eleven. On weekends I was allowed to stay out till one o'clock, but I had to sign in when I came back. And if I wanted to go someplace for a weekend, say, I couldn't just go. I needed the permission of my house mother.

Oh, that was nothing! There were rules and rules for girls. I don't know if anybody ever wrote them down, but every girl knew these rules by heart, anyway. Such as: You speak in a low voice. You don't act smart around boys. Let the *man* take the lead. And don't, above all, *don't* have sex before you're married. That was the way to perdition. [Laughs] If you could follow all those rules, you were considered a "nice girl" who'd be married before the dangerous old age of twenty-two!

Well, of course we all wanted to be nice, but, lord, it was so hard! You just couldn't be yourself. A little for-instance—I loved wearing jeans. Wore them with the cuffs rolled up and with a big man's shirt tied at the

waist. Well, that was all right for weekends, but for school—forget it! It had to be stockings and skirts and little strings of fake pearls. Ladylike, you know.

And if you were the least bit plump—and I was, for a while—under that skirt you wore a girdle. Oh! Just thinking of that girdle gives me the willies. A torture garment. As for your— What do you kids call them now? Your boobs—there wasn't a girl I knew, including me, who wasn't miserable about what she had. Either too much or too little, according to some mystical idea of perfection. I mean, *male* idea of perfection! We all felt such pressure to be perfect! And to catch a man! *That*, after all, was the big goal. Success in life. [Laughs]

Listen, every night I rolled my hair up on metal curlers and then slept on those hunks of metal. More torture. But, heavens, you couldn't go to school with straight hair! Everything really was so much more rigid and codified. That's what appealed to me about Eric.

To begin with, he looked like an Eric—beautiful, Nordic, Viking type. He'd been in the army, he'd been to college (on the GI Bill), and he'd done this absolutely incredible thing of getting a degree, and *then not using it*. From college, with his precious bachelor of arts degree, he'd become a bus driver!

Now this bus he was driving happened to stop right in front of Rader's Cut Rite Drugs at least four times every day. And he would come in, buy a candy bar, or a newspaper. You know. It wasn't long before we went from joking over the counter to going out on dates. Oh, I was just dazzled. Eric was different from any of the boys I knew. He had ambition, but it wasn't the ambition to be a professional and make boodles of money. His ambition was to be a union organizer. And more than that, he had *principles*. Socialist principles. He wanted to change society. Change people. Change the way things were done. I had never heard such ideas— the workers taking over the factories and having the profits, instead of the owners? And the words he used! Today, everyone uses words like *establishment, power structure,* and *the military-industrial complex*. But back then? I'd never heard things like that. Eric's very favorite word, though, was *bourgeois*.

I can still remember his saying to me, "Zel, your father is a worker, but *you* are bourgeois to your soul." It was the *worst* thing he could call anyone! It meant having middle-class values. Being concerned about things like getting a college degree and worrying about my appearance.

He was right about me. [Laughs] I was trying so hard to be nice, to get ahead, to do all these things. And what for? According to Eric, so I could leave the working class, which he spoke of as "noble" (as well as "exploited"), and become one of those people who lived a smug, self-satisfied life of materialistic values!

Furthermore, he said, when you got right down to it, the most bourgeois aspect of my behavior was my attitude about sex. To put it bluntly, Eric wanted to make love, and I was resisting. Naturally! I was a nice girl! Everything I'd been taught was that nice girls *didn't*, not until they got married.

I remember one day, after the usual push-pull, Eric blurting out, "You must think it's property. You act like an incipient capitalist, hoarding his stake. I guess," he said, "it's going to take you a lot longer to get rid of your false bourgeois attitudes."

I just didn't know what to say. I was crushed by his remarks. He sounded so reproachful, so regretful, so *sad*.

I'm sure that was the moment when I decided that if I couldn't live up to Eric's standards one way, I'd do it another way. I'd find a factory job and become one of the "oppressed masses" he revered.

My parents were stunned by my decision not to go back to school that fall. But I guess some things never change. When you're nineteen and think you're in love, you're not listening to your parents.

Anyway, the first place I tried, MIF, Mica Insulating Factory, hired me. Just like that. Couldn't believe it. Someone from personnel pointed me across a yard to the Women's Building and told me to find Eddy, the foreman, and give him my hiring slip.

The Women's Building was concrete with steel doors. I swear the walls actually quivered from the sound of what seemed to me to be a thousand presses. I found the foreman at the far end of this huge, noisy

room near a stand-up desk. He took the hiring slip.
"Your name is Zelda?" he shouted. I didn't like his
eyes—they were like little dirty pebbles—and I didn't
like the way he looked me over with those eyes.

"You fast?" he shouted. I nodded. "Not afraid to
work?" He wrote something on a dirty yellow legal
pad clipped to a dirty clipboard. Everything was dirty
in that place—the floor, the walls, Eddy's fingernails,
the windows, his desk.

Oh, I should qualify that. The women who worked
there—they *sparkled*. They dressed like gypsies or
dancers, with big hoop earrings, and scarves over their
hair, and swirly skirts and bright blouses.

Anyway, Eddy gave me a shove and pointed me
toward Florry on number-ten machine. Florry was
English, she was redheaded, she was about my
mother's age, and she was a great woman. I found her
sitting like a queen in front of her machine, her back
straight as a ruler. I stood and watched her for a
moment. Her hands moved so beautifully, so fast, she
was so perfectly coordinated with the machine that I
knew I'd never be able to compare.

I tapped her on the shoulder and yelled that Eddy
had sent me. "New girl?" she said. "Watch, now."

From a basket near her left foot she took a handful
of mica fragments, dropped them on the machine
counter, slipped one golden brown chip under the
machine arm, and pressed a lever with her other foot.
The huge heavy arm came down—*WHANG!* It was
the sound of those machine arms, fifty of them, coming

down second after second that filled the air with such a thick, deafening din.

The arm came down on the mica and a round disc with a serrated edge was stamped out. Florry moved the mica, down came the arm—she did that again and once more. Got four cuts out of that one piece. A little like cutting cookie dough. Only with cookie dough, if you press the cutter too close to the edge and don't make a perfect round, you can still bake the cookie. Here, you could keep only the perfect cuts, which were then pushed down a chute in back of the machine. The pieces you messed up went into a scrap basket. And you didn't make any money on them.

"That's it," Florry mouthed to me, after showing me the procedure a couple more times. "Go to it." She nodded to the empty machine next to hers.

I sat down on the iron stool, turned on the power, and watched the belt slipping around the arm. I was terrified as I slid the first piece of yellow mica under the arm and pressed the lever foot. *WHANG!* I had good reason to be scared. You could lose your fingers, with no trouble at all, to that arm. In fact, there were several three- and four-fingered women working in the building.

WHANG! WHANG! WHANG! My foot slipped and I punched the mica three times without moving it around. I'd ruined the piece. I looked around, afraid Eddy was watching. He was! My face burned, my hands were damp. Oh, I was sweating. Those first hours I must have lost five pounds just from anxiety.

At noon a whistle shrilled and the machines shut down. My head felt numb in the silence. Then the quiet was broken again, but this time by the more pleasant sounds of fifty women laughing and talking, rushing toward the time clock.

Florry caught my arm and pulled me into the mass of women carrying sweaters, newspapers, lunch bags, and Thermoses. "Come along, girl! Did you bring your lunch? Hurry now, luv. We don't have that much time. Twenty minutes."

As it turned out, more than enough for me. The moment Florry led me into the "lunchroom," I lost my appetite. Flaking vomit-green walls. Scabby-looking linoleum underfoot. And then the dandiest feature of the "ladies' lounge"—a flimsy, shoulder-high partition separating those eating lunch from those using the row of toilet stalls.

The room was packed. Women leaned against the walls, squeezed onto a cracked brown leather couch and a couple of chairs, squatted on the floor, and sat in each other's laps.

"Girls!" I noticed how everyone stopped talking to listen to Florry. "This is Zelda, the new girl on number nine."

"Hi, Zelda, welcome to the zoo."

"Zelda, cute name!"

"Think you're going to like it here?"

The calls and shouts came from all over. I smiled. "Hi! I guess it's going to be fun working here."

You should have heard them then. Catcalls, hoots, laughter, groans.

A toilet flushed and I asked Florry if you could eat outside. "Certainly, luv."

"Don't do it," someone said. "It makes you koo-koo."

"Aww, she'll go koo-koo just working here."

"You wanna try the prison yard, honey, you try it. It's great, ha ha."

"Whatsa matter? You don't like our ladies' lounge? This place is just like home, ain't it, girls?"

I smiled from one to the other. I didn't have them sorted out yet into names to go with faces.

"She's cute," someone said about me, "but she don't look old enough to even have her working papers." This made me blush. My round baby face was always embarrassing me.

"You got a boyfriend, Zelda?" That was Carmella, a skinny imp with a cloud of dark hair and eyes that danced mischievously behind thick lenses. She and I got friendly, but that day I just didn't know what to say when she went on, "Your boyfriend do you yet?" I blushed even harder.

"Aww, leave the nice baby alone." Then a loud happy laugh. And that was how I first picked Adelina out of the crowd. She was a little soft-looking woman with huge dark popping eyes. A sweetiepie. Her husband had left her, she was raising four kids alone, she'd lost a home to fire and one child to polio, but she had the biggest, freshest, loudest, happiest laugh

I can ever remember hearing. When Adelina laughed —and all sorts of things struck her funny—it was irresistible.

It seemed I'd hardly found a corner of a chair to sit on, had hardly begun talking to Adelina and Carmella, when the whistle blew. Everyone rushed for the door, scrambling to be first at the time clock. "You get docked half an hour if you're more than five minutes late," Florry explained, pulling me along by the arm. "Hurry!"

Hurry! Hurry! Hurry! That was the pace of life in MIF. Wake up in the morning and hurry to work! Rush that mica through the machine! Got to make the rate! Hurry to the lunchroom! Hurry back! Get to work!

Every night I was exhausted, aching. I'd never worked like this in my life. My parents watched me and said little. I think, now, that they were just waiting for me to get over my romantic ideas about the glories of factory life.

As for Eric—couldn't have been more pleased! He was in his element, educating me, lecturing, pointing out to me that I had a unique opportunity. "These are the most downtrodden workers, Zelda. The unorganized. They are the most grossly exploited. You can help them understand that they can take their destinies into their own hands. They need to be organized."

I didn't disagree about that, but I didn't think I could educate anyone in that shop to anything. As for "downtrodden," that just made me laugh. Carmella?

Adelina? Florry? *Downtrodden?* They worked twice as fast as I did, twice as hard, and they could still sing, scream jokes to each other, and notice every man who came into the shop.

Machines were always breaking down. "Number twenny-three down," someone would yell. A mechanic came running, and the bawdy remarks flew through the air.

"Oh, lord, he's so sweet," Carmella caroled.

"Do you think he's taken?" From another side of the room.

"Come here and see *me*, honey. I'm sure something's wrong with my machine that *you* can fix."

And I just listened, laughing, blushing. They dubbed me "the baby." Why not? I was so naive. After working two weeks, my first paycheck thrilled me. "Look at all this money," I said to Carmella. "This is great."

"Ain't nothing great but loving," Carmella assured me, as if I were about twenty years younger than she was, instead of only two.

In fact, on Friday, when pay envelopes were opened, there was gloom in the lunchroom. Friday was the worst day of the week. Friday was when people found out if they made their piecework rate.

Here's how that worked. A price was put on each little piece stamped out on the press. It might be an eighth of a cent if the die, the pattern, was tiny, or as much as a penny if the die was large. The smallest dies paid the least because you could get the most cuts from a single piece of mica. So, the theory was, it was an advantage. Whip that piece around, get eight cuts, and make that penny just as fast as someone with a large penny die.

But, in fact, the eighth of a cent or the quarter of a cent was earned only on good cuts. And how you got good cuts depended on lots of things. To begin with— pray for Eddy to deliver you a load of mica neither too thick nor too brittle. Pray for your machine not to break down. Pray you could keep that machine *WHANG! WHANG! WHANG! WHANG! WHANG-ING!* as fast as it could go. Never think about the fingers that had been lost to the machine. Never slack off. And, on a good day, you might make as much as a dollar and a half an hour. If you could do that every day, then there'd be sixty dollars in the pay packet. That was a lot of money. A powerful lot of money! Everyone was always trying for the big sixty. But only a few of Eddy's pets ever made it.

For every good day when an operator made that kind of money, there were the other days when she made forty or fifty cents an hour. And on Friday, gloomy Friday, nearly everyone ended with a little more or a little less than forty dollars for forty hours of work.

A month passed. I was learning. No longer so glowing about facing that punch press every day. Amazed, abashed, to learn that Adelina had worked there for ten years, Carmella for four, Florry for five. And had no idea of ever working anywhere else.

"Well, well? Are you talking to them about the union?" Eric prodded me.

I mumbled something. He had such a—such a *false* idea of what I could do. What *could* I do? I was green, I was raw, I didn't know half what anyone else in that place knew about what it meant to work, to be underpaid, and still hold up your head.

Then, in a manner I could never have foreseen, I *did* have something to do with changing things in MIF. It was totally accidental.

I remember, one day, Carmella's asking me if Eddy had been bothering me. Well, he did hang around my machine a lot, but I thought he was just checking my work.

Carmella linked arms with me. "Watch out for him, he's got roaming hands."

"Oh, I can take care of myself," I said quickly. I certainly felt like a big well-fed horse next to skinny Carm.

She laughed at me. She knew me better than I knew me. "If he tries anything, you just tell him—" And she chopped her right hand into the crook of her left elbow.

A few nights later I showed Eric the arm salute, proud of everything I was learning, of my independence, of my new swaggering style—gypsy skirts, bright scarves around my hair, and big hoop earrings. I'd had my ears pierced. Carmella had done it in the lunchroom. Put an ice cube on my earlobe, held it there for a moment, then punched a needle through the lobe and left a silk thread in the hole.

"You've changed," Eric said. Did he sound a bit miffed? "I never thought you'd do it, you know. Go into the factory that way. And—" He looked at me, almost helplessly. "And *everything*."

"I know. You thought I was too *bourgeois*." I stuck out my tongue, like Angie, the new bride that everyone teased. And I gave him the arm salute again.

"You're really getting *sassy*," he said.

Sure I was! It was the influence of my new friends, my new world. I felt as if my parents had been keeping a secret from me all these years. I'd always felt sorry for them, having to go to work in a factory every day. But now it turned out they must have been having fun, too.

One night Eric and I parked. We talked about the shop first—that was "business"—then got into our inevitable hassle over how far we were going to "go." "You're still so backward," he said at last, giving up. He frowned handsomely, smoking and looking out the window.

"I'm sorry," I said.

"I don't see much of you anymore, either," he complained.

"I know. I'm sorry. I'm so tired at night." Why did I keep saying to him that I was sorry? Sorry I couldn't make love. Sorry I wasn't on call. Sorry I was so ignorant. Sorry I hadn't already converted everyone in MIF to union thoughts. I made up my mind that before I said "sorry" once more to Eric, I'd sooner cut out my tongue.

So there we sat, Eric sulking, me silent. I kept staring at his wonderful Viking profile. It didn't seem to matter so much, anymore, that he was so attractive. The truth was, I realized, I thought more about the women I worked with than I did about him. And then I surprised myself again by thinking that I loved my shop friends more, *much more*, than Eric. Now *that* was a revolutionary thought. Don't forget, the general idea then was that the company of any man (not even to speak of an exceptional one like Eric) was infinitely preferable to the company of *any* woman, no matter how interesting or lively. Oh, yeah? [Laughs] Wanna bet?

Well, a few days later, I was a little slow leaving my machine at lunchtime. I was mulling over Eric and where we were headed. Before I knew it, the room had emptied, Eddy loomed up, and yes, indeed, he did have roaming hands. I know it's a cliché, but my heart was pounding so hard with shock, I really thought it was going to break through my chest. I don't know if I said anything to him, pushed him away, or just ran for my life.

The next thing I remember is bursting into the lunchroom, and little fat Mary Margaret, with her mouth full of food, saying, "Look at Zelda, look at Zelda, her face is all red."

Everyone stopped talking and looked at me.

"What happened, baby?" Adelina asked me in her husky voice.

"Eddy—" I gulped. All I could get out was his name. Didn't want to cry, but the tears flowed anyway.

"Eddy, huh!" Carmella patted my back.

Everyone seemed to know without another word what it meant.

"Gee, don't cry," Mary Margaret said, "we all been felt up when we didn't wanna be."

That made me cry harder. And, with that, Angie, our bride, put her apron over her face and started to cry, too! It seemed that the day before, when she was at her machine, Eddy had put his hand up her skirt.

"Men! They're all alike," Adelina said hoarsely. "But that Eddy is a real dog," she added.

"He's got no right," Angie bawled. "I didn't give him the right."

"Girls!" Florry sat up straight. "It's a bloody shame when kids like Angie and Zelda can't do a day's work without being molested." Her voice rose over Angie's bawling. "We don't belong to Eddy. We don't belong to the company. Just because we work here, break our backs for pennies—!"

"Ain't it the truth," someone sighed.

Florry's head snapped around. "Isn't it bloody disgusting what we work for? Isn't it bloody disgusting that we have to eat in this little pokehole?"

There were murmurs around the room. Agreement or disagreement? I couldn't tell. My tears had dried up.

Florry stood up, put her hands on hips, and turned to look at each and every woman. When she had our attention, she said slowly, "Let's do something for ourselves, *for once*. Stick together, *for once*."

"What can we do?" a voice bleated.

Just then the whistle blew. There was the usual stirring, women standing, smoothing their hair, crumpling lunch bags. "Girls!" Florry raised her voice. "Why don't we *sit right here* until bloody Eddy bloody promises to keep his hands to himself!"

"You mean not go back to our machines?" Mary Margaret squeaked. "Not go back to *work*?"

"That's what I mean."

For a moment the room went quiet with shock. Then came the protests, a hubbub of sound. "We can't do that!" "They'll *fire* us." "I need my job."

"Fire us?" Florry sniffed scornfully. "There are thirty bloody three of us here! They're not going to fire thirty-three operators. Girls, do we or don't we have backbone?"

Someone crunched an apple. A toilet flushed. And everyone looked at everyone else. Then the door burst open. Not even a knock, and Eddy was inside, pulling at his greasy hair, screaming. "What the hell is going on? You girls know what time it is?" He showed his yellow teeth in a snarl. "Get back to work!"

Carmella jumped up, crossing her matchstick arms, skinny elbows sticking out. "Why don't you keep your paws to yourself," she screeched. "We know what you did to Zelda and Angie."

"Shut up, you! Now, haul ass back to them machines, or you're all fired." He grabbed Carmella, who was half his size, and started dragging her toward the door. That was a mistake. Adelina rushed to Carmella's rescue. Then Florry. In another moment Eddy was surrounded by women screaming at him and dragging poor Carm away. A wonder her arms weren't broken.

"You creep!" I could hear Adelina's husky voice over everyone else's. "You Jack the Ripper!" Her eyes were nearly popping out of her head. "You dirty old thing." Then the clincher. "What'samatter, brother, you can't get it at home?" And she gave one of her loud, joyous laughs.

Eddy turned brick-red. "I give you five minutes," he yelled over the pandemonium, "or the whole bunch of you is out on the sidewalk." He slammed out.

Well, then the *silence*. Like they say, you could have cut it with a knife. Adelina collapsed into a chair with a deep, sad sigh. After a bit she said, "Well, we had our fun, so now let's forget it. You girls know I got to support my kids. I can't afford to lose my job. None of us can."

Three or four women slipped out. There was a general stir. Carmella nursed her bruised arm. "Girls," Florry said quietly, "if we give in now, Eddy will be worse than ever. He'll know we're scared of him. I'm ready to sit. Is anyone else?"

Silence again. And again everyone looked at everyone else. Waiting for the other person to make the first move one way or the other, to say the first word. Then, of all people, little fat Mary Margaret, looking half scared to death, stood up, said, "I'll do it!" and collapsed back into her seat, pudgy hands clasped at her heart.

We all stared at Mary Margaret, who, up till that moment, had made her chief claim to fame on eating three bananas every day for lunch. Adelina whistled through her teeth. Carmella gave a raucous laugh. "Hey! I ain't gonna be shamed by Mary. I'll stay, too." She swaggered over to the couch.

Another few women left. Florry, like an avenging redheaded goddess, once again looked eye-to-eye with each woman. I could feel the tension, the nervousness, in the air, like strings being drawn across my skin. Were we going to stay? Or were we going to give in to Eddy?

Reve Fernmaker, a big motherly woman, tucked her gray hair back into its bun and cleared her throat. Heads swiveled. "Well," Reve said comfortably, "I need my job, too." She smoothed her apron. "But—I'm for staying."

A deep sigh seemed to pass around the room, from woman to woman. Without another word of discussion everyone settled down. "What now?" Francie said. She was a pretty girl with a little cupid's-bow mouth. Wore a whole lot of makeup, and supported herself and her boyfriend with her job at MIF and yodeling on weekends in bars. "What happens now?"

The same question we all had.

What happened was that fifteen minutes later Eddy was back. "Move, you pigs! Get to them machines!"

My God, I've never seen anyone so furious in my life. I thought he'd have a stroke on the spot. His face was boiling, twice its normal size. "Move!" He was screaming, out of control.

"We ain't moving," Adelina said. "We want some changes around here."

"We—ain't—moving!" Francie, the yodeler, chanted it, softly clapping her hands. And everyone took it up.

"We ain't moving! We ain't moving! We ain't moving!" We pounded our feet on the floor. "We ain't moving!"

We sat in the lunchroom all afternoon, talking and singing. Francie yodeled for us, did her nightclub act, and we all applauded, stamped, and whistled. I remember we sang popular songs, too, especially "Riders in the Sky." Everyone was singing that one, that year. It was Vaughn Monroe's big hit.

And every time Eddy stuck his head in the door and screamed at us pigs to get back to them machines, we laughed in his face. I remember Carmella saying, "How come we dopes didn't ever do this sooner?"

One time when Eddy came in, Reve, the motherly one, went nose to nose with him and said very quietly, "And don't you call us 'girls' in that tone of voice, mister. We are *women*. We are grown-up women, and we demand some *respect*." It was a wonderful moment. I still get chills down my back, remembering.

Around four o'clock the company supervisor

appeared. One of the big shots and quite a different person from Eddy. A handsome, silvery-haired man wearing a sweater and a tie. Very relaxed, easy, sympathetic. He listened to the complaints Florry listed, nodding, giving warm, fatherly looks. Florry spoke about the rates, Eddy's roaming hands, and the ugliness of our lunchroom.

"I don't blame you ladies for being upset," he said. He made promises. A new lunchroom, longer lunch hour, and as for Eddy, he said flatly, "You won't have any trouble with him, again."

When he left, we all did, too. We thought we had won. Eddy watched us go, stood there, saying nothing, his hands in his pockets. After all the exhilaration, all the emotion, the singing and shouting, we left quietly, arms around each other. I felt wonderful—powerful, maybe, for the first time in my life.

The very next day, the lunchroom was painted a sunny yellow. Two days later three new chairs appeared. "You see what happens when we stick together," Florry said. And Carmella said, "Ain't it the truth!" Then, on Friday, when we got our pay packets, Eddy told Adelina, Carmella, Florry, and me not to bother coming back. Fired. All of us, fired for being troublemakers.

Everyone watched us leave. Everyone knew about the firings. That was the point—to scare all the other women into being "good" again. Florry was just sick about how we'd been taken in by the company supervisor. "That bloody smooth-talking bloody man!"

Adelina was pretty upset, too, afraid she wouldn't find another job.

Well, all of us managed to find work. We kept in touch the next few months. I went to work in a box factory, putting together cardboard boxes. [Laughs] Someone has to do that, you know. And then I had a job sewing baseballs and, for a short while, I worked as a chambermaid in a hotel. It was never the same as working in MIF, though. Never the same as working with Florry, Carmella, and Adelina.

By the time fall rolled around, I was ready to go back to school. And I did. And—you know how these things are—I didn't forget my friends, but now our lives were so different.

Well, over winter vacation I was home, and I ran into Mary Margaret. We went into a White Tower and had hamburgers, and she told me that right after the firings there'd been talk about getting in the union. But it died down when the company promised to review the piecework rate, to increase paid holidays, and give ten days a year sick leave.

In fact, though, it was all talk. Nothing had changed. Everything was back to "normal." Except now, a lot of women were for the union—they realized that without a union they had no power whatsoever. But no one dared come out in the open and say this. Not if they wanted to keep their jobs.

After that I didn't hear anything for a couple more years. Then the strangest coincidence—the same month I graduated from college my mother sent me news that there had been (for the second time) an NLRB election in the plant, and this time the union had won. I burst into tears. I remember exactly how I felt, what I thought. *At last! At last. A victory for the girls.*

So, that's pretty much the end of the story. Oh, one other point I was thinking about as I was telling you all this. You notice how we called ourselves and each other "girls"? And remember when Reve Fernmaker stood up to Eddy and told him we were *women*? I don't think there's really any contradiction there.

We didn't say "sisters" then, the way some women do today. But I think calling each other "girls" was a kind of substitute for that. Sometimes it was ironic. Sometimes affectionate. But, always, there was all the difference in the world between the way *we* said it to one another, and the way Eddy or any other man said it to *us*.

Well, that really is the end of my story. Unless you want to know about Eric and me. That's history, too, isn't it? Even if, of a lesser kind. What happened was —we just saw less and less of each other. No longer found each other so interesting. I wonder if Eric even remembers me anymore. I can just see him wrinkling his handsome brow and saying, "Zelda Sagan? Zelda Sagan? Hmm. . . ." [Laughs] Of course I've never forgotten him. But not for his darling handsome face. Oh, no. What I've never forgotten is that except for Eric, I would never have known Carmella, Adelina, and Florry.

Amelia Earhart, Where Are You When I Need You?

Of course I had heard my parents talking about my crazy aunt, nearly always in whispers behind closed doors. Aunt Clare was my mother's sister and she was peculiar. Once, she'd gone to the drugstore wearing nothing but a raincoat and clogs. Another time she'd invited people to a party, then locked them out, yelling at them to go away and stop bothering her.

Clare lived alone in another city, and about once a month, my mother (her only relative, as Clare was my only relative, aside from my parents)—my mother phoned her. I would hear my mother say, "Clare?" in a special rising, extra-bright voice. "How are you?" "Do you need anything? . . . Money, or . . ."

Then she would listen for a long time, saying, "Uh

huh . . . well . . . yes . . ." And, finally, she would say, "Don't forget, if you need anything, Paul and I are right here." And she would hang up the phone and fall into a chair with a sigh, saying, "Ah, well . . ."

I sensed my mother's mingled shame and sorrow over her sister, but I had very little curiosity. Never having seen Clare—except when I was an infant, which I couldn't remember—she didn't seem real to me. If I felt anything about her, it was a sort of shallow pride. In exactly the same way I might announce to a friend that my father had a real World War II German pistol, or that my mother, a language teacher, was sometimes asked to interpret Spanish in court, I would say, "*I* have a crazy aunt." Top *that* if you can.

Then one summer my father needed an operation that had to be performed at a famous clinic in Kansas. My mother was going with him and, for lack of any other place, I would board with my aunt for the three weeks my parents were to be gone.

Everything was arranged swiftly. Time was important for my father and so my parents saw me off on the bus to my aunt's on the same day they flew to Kansas. "You'll be all right, darling?" my mother said.

I hung out the window, nodding, feeling a little numb. This would be my first real separation from my parents.

"Don't forget to practice your clarinet," my mother urged. I nodded again. My parents were both teachers and we lived a calm, ordered life. They had spoken to me about keeping to a schedule (go to bed on time, rise at a reasonable hour), being responsible (wash your dishes, don't make work for your Aunt Clare), and doing such things as writing them regularly and practicing the clarinet an hour every day.

The bus started. "Good-bye." I stretched out my hand, still not able to believe in my father's illness. He was so large, so robust, so healthy-looking with his square tortoiseshell glasses and his firm paunch beneath a green shirt. He waved to me—they both did, my mother throwing kisses—until the bus turned the corner.

My aunt met me at the bus station. Had she had a large sign on her chest with her name, CRAZY CLARE, painted on it, I would not have recognized her any more swiftly. As I stepped into the smoky station and looked around at the crowds milling between the doors, I saw her at once. A long-faced woman wearing a full orange skirt made of some crinkly papery material and a pink T-shirt with red letters: BURNING BUSH BANK CELEBRATES. On her feet, sneakers and white ankle socks. I stood frozen, clutching my suitcase, but she had spotted me.

"Phoebe? You look just like Sally." I nodded mutely, and followed her out into the street. "It's not a long walk. Do you mind?" I walked next to her, but not quite, a half-step behind, as if I really weren't with her. She moved along briskly. I kept stealing glances. Her eyes were huge and dark, and her hair, with an astounding energy of its own, sprang out in sharp crackling curls all over her head. She had two or three combs stuck in here and there, but none seemed to have the least effect in keeping her hair tamed.

It was her eyes I kept returning to, somehow unlike the eyes of any adult I knew. They were full of a shimmering, moving light, and at the same time were so deeply black that I, at once, remembered a moment, long ago, when I had gazed into the long, secret depths of a well. I must have been very small. I remembered the beating of my heart as I stared into the thick, dark waters, and then my mother's hands lifting me up, taking me away from the danger.

Clare lived in the attic apartment of an old wooden building on Greene Street. We went up three flights of roofed-over outside steps, past other people's back porches. To my surprise, the apartment—three very small rooms—was furnished in a decorous, almost timid manner: a worn couch and two chairs facing each other in a perfect little square, the bed made up with a wrinkleless tufted spread, the Formica kitchen table holding only a red plastic napkin holder and a pair of glass salt and pepper shakers. I suppose I had thought I would step into some wild Halloween disorder.

"Are you hungry?" Clare said. We had hardly spoken on the walk from the bus station. "I bet you're hungry."

I shook my head and put down my suitcase and clarinet. My mother had packed me a lunch, but sheer terror of what lay ahead had destroyed my appetite.

"Well, then," she said, sitting up very straight across from me at the kitchen table. "So you're Phoebe, my baby niece."

"Yes," I said miserably. I couldn't think of anything else to say. It seemed impossible that I would find anything to ever say until the long, long three weeks of my stay were over.

I watched Clare carefully, waiting for her to make her craziness known. I sat on the edge of the chair, only my toes meeting the floor, ready for flight. I expected anything: At any moment might she not spring up and whirl around the room screeching in a language no one had ever heard? Or, eyes glittering, leap at me with the knife she had taken up to slice into a hunk of cheese?

"Umm, good," she said, patting her belly. "Want some?"

Cautiously, I ate a bit of the cheese (afraid to keep saying no) and when, in a while, she said maybe I should go to bed, the trip must have been tiring, I rose with relief, my knees limp. Yes, she was right, I was exhausted.

Lying in the unfamiliar bed, clutching a sneaker as a weapon, and listening to the unfamiliar noises of the street far below, I longed with a hot, excruciating ache in my chest for my own room with its shelves full of books and model planes, its soft shaggy yellow rug, and the poster of Amelia Earhart in her flier's cap, on the wall opposite my bed, where I could see her clear, brave flier's eyes the moment I woke up.

I had often told myself to be brave like Amelia. Whenever something difficult faced me—a test, a dentist's appointment, a fight with a friend—I whispered my secret words. *Amelia Earhart . . . Amelia Earhart . . .* In the last year or so I had become aware that, while I lived with my parents in a kind of calm sea of love and safety, the world at large was a different affair, a boiling ocean with scummy, white-capped waves. Still, it had had nothing to do with me. Until now. Suddenly, it seemed, I had been dumped into that ocean. Sink or swim.

I planned to stay awake and alert all night. No knowing what a crazy person would do. At every sound the hair on the back of my neck stiffened. Floors groaned, the walls rustled, and outside my room I heard Clare walking and muttering to herself. My hand was rigid on the sneaker. I still held it when I woke in the morning.

I lay in bed for a while, listening. The quiet disturbed me as much as the sounds of the night before. Tiptoeing, I cracked open the door and peeked into the kitchen. No Clare. My heart pounding, I shuffled silently across the cool linoleum to the living room. No Clare. She was gone. Or was she? I stared at a closed closet door. Was she hiding inside? That would certainly be a crazy thing to do.

Wiping my hands on my pajamas, I called, "Clare? Aunt Clare?" I knocked on the door. "Hiii!" I said in an extra-friendly way. "I'm up. You in there?" I waited a moment, then gripped the knob. "I'm going to open the door now," I said in a loud, bright voice. "Okay? I'm going to open it. Ready or not," I called coyly, and yanked the door open.

Hangers clanked in the draft. A raincoat and a hooded sweat shirt nodded peacefully. On the floor high rubber boots, red sneakers, and two pairs of scuffed oxfords were lined up in precise rows. An umbrella leaned against the wall.

Clare was definitely gone. But suddenly I had another disturbing idea. What if she had locked me in? I rushed to the front door. It *was* locked! I yanked at it, my hands slippery on the knob. Then, after a moment of panic and hard breathing, I saw a key on a nail. A little round tag attached to it said PHOEBE. I put it into the keyhole and unlocked the door. The hall was dim, the staircase shadowy. Was someone breathing quietly out there? Quickly, I locked myself in again.

"At least I know you're not hiding in here, Aunt Clare," I said. The sound of my own voice comforted me. "I'm hungry," I said out loud, going into the kitchen. "What do you have to eat?"

Not much. A chunk of stale bologna, last night's cheese, two black, overripe bananas that went to mush in my hands when I peeled them, a box of crackers, and a pot of cold congealed oatmeal. Well, I was hungry enough to eat *anything*, but crazy people stories were crackling in my head: razor blades in Halloween apples, poisoned milk, mice in soup.

I tackled one of the black bananas, broke the soft

fruit into mushy chunks and, after smelling it, ate it cautiously with little motions of teeth and tongue, probing for poison, for splinters of metal. I finished off the second banana, then ate the crackers, pawing them out of the box and washing them down with water.

I brushed my teeth, dressed, made the bed, and wrote my parents a letter about how much fun the bus trip had been. "Aunt Clare is very—" I paused, then wrote "—unusual and interesting. This morning for breakfast I had sliced bananas and all the Ritz crackers I could eat, two of my favorite things!" I wrote large and filled an entire page, putting in lots of exclamation points so they'd know I was happy, and not worry.

I played my clarinet for a while; at home my father always put his hands over his ears when I hit a bad note, and groaned loudly.

I drifted around the apartment, breathing heavily. Not even noon yet. The air inside was dim, stuffy. Dust danced in the windows. Drifting past the tiny kitchen window, I saw a boy in red shorts down below in the backyard. He squatted, grabbed a set of barbells, and lifted. Squinting my eyes, I imagined I could see the sheen of sweat on his bare smooth chest. He had long legs.

"Yum yum, cutesy legs," I said. It was strange watching him and knowing he didn't know he was being watched. Once a girl friend and I had screamed at a strange boy, "You are sexy and *adorable!*" Then we had run away, laughing and gasping and hitting each other on the arms.

I was lying on the bed, wishing I were someplace else, when I heard noises in the hall. I sat up, grabbed a sneaker, then a book. My heart shoved up into my throat. Scuffling noises at the door. Door opening. Voices—one loud and nasty, one high and ironic. I slid my legs off the bed. Lock myself in? Confront them? Throw the book at one intruder and hit the other in the belly with my sneaker? Gulping, clutching sneaker and book, I shuffled toward the kitchen.

My aunt appeared, holding a grocery bag and talking to herself. "Just do that over again, will you, dear?" (The loud, nasty voice.) "Do it over? Why certainly, *madam*. Anything you say, *madam*." (The high ironic voice.) "I hate to ask you this, dear . . ." "Oh, I know how you hate to ask me *anything*. You're every inch *consideration*." Over the top of the grocery bag her face worked: she scowled, twisted her lips, flared her nostrils scornfully. Expressions flashed, one after the other, like storm clouds across the sky.

She dumped the grocery bag on the table. She wore a T-shirt and jeans. Her hair was pulled back with a rubber band, but still sprang out of bounds.

"Hello, Aunt Clare," I said.

She spun around. "Phoebe?" she said quickly.

I nodded. My heart was still jumping about in an irregular way.

"Three weeks," she said, as if we were in the middle

of a conversation. "Is that it? Three weeks?" And she made a grotesque face, like a child, screwing down her mouth and crinkling her forehead so that her eyes almost disappeared. And then she shut her eyes entirely, as if the thought of the three weeks with me frightened her beyond words.

Later, when we were eating the spaghetti she had fixed, she asked me if I liked my name. "Fee-bee," she said on two notes, like a birdcall. "Do you like that name?"

No one had ever asked me. In fact I had often wished for a name like Jamie or Toby or Wendy. Or if it had to be something like Phoebe, why couldn't it have been Amelia?

"Phoebe is a bird name," Clare said. "Phoebe bird, Phoebe bird, Phoebe bird. Phoebe bird, what do you think of the name *Clare*?"

"Fine," I muttered.

"Phoebe says Clare's name is fine," she mimicked. "Little liar!" Then she really frightened me by looking into my mind and saying, "What are you afraid of, Phoebe?"

"Nothing," I said numbly.

"Liar," she said again. "Liar, and *dope*," she added calmly. She leaned so close to me that I closed my eyes so as not to fall into hers. "You don't have to be afraid of me," she said. "Better look around and see what you really ought to be afraid of."

"What?" I whispered. "What do you mean? What should I be afraid of?"

There was a half-smile, triumphant and knowing, on her face. "Everything," she said. "*Everything.*"

The next morning, again Clare was gone before I was out of bed. And, again, I prowled the apartment, even to opening the closet door with many loud cheerful cries. Empty. "You're acting crazy," I told myself. And I decided I would not talk to myself, but the silence of the apartment weighed on me. Before long I was consulting myself about everything. "Cold spaghetti for breakfast? Oh, well, why not." "Wonder if the boy in the red shorts is coming out again. Nope, not there yet." "Check the kitchen window—oh, goody, there he is."

Aunt Clare returned in the middle of the afternoon with groceries again. Since she was crazy, I believed she spent all that time buying food, and cautiously I asked if it was hard for her to make up her mind.

"Why?" she said, pouring a glass of milk.

"Well . . . because . . . uh . . . it takes quite a while," I said delicately.

"It doesn't take me any time at all to shop." She pantomimed snatching cans and boxes off the shelves at a great rate. "But you have trouble making up your mind?" she said, as if sympathizing with a private nuttiness of mine that she didn't share, but would try to understand.

This irritated me. "If you're not shopping, where do you go in the morning?" I said, abandoning delicacy.

"To work."

"Where?"

"Everywhere." She grabbed a broom and danced with it. "Everywhere and somewhere and nowhere and here and there and yonder and so forth," she sang, dancing with the broom. "Get it?"

I shook my head and she sighed. "What do you do with a broom? Clean. Right? That's the clue, Phoebe bird. I clean with brooms and mops and rags and buckets."

"You clean *what*?"

"Houses."

"Houses?"

"Now you've got it." She narrowed her eyes, tapping her forehead with a single finger to tell me I was catching on fast.

"Why couldn't you just say so in the first place?"

"Because it wouldn't have been as much fun." She stuck out her tongue at me.

Oh, God. She was so *childish*. Childish and crazy.

"Now why don't you ask me if I like cleaning house, like your mother asks me all the time. 'Clare, you could do something better with yourself,'" she said in an eerie imitation of my mother's falsely cheerful once-a-month telephone voice. Her face twisted. "Cleaning houses is good. People leave me alone. *They* don't know how to clean worth a shirt. Cleaning makes me strong." Pushing up her sleeve, she showed me the muscles in her arm. "Feel it, go ahead, squeeze it," she demanded. Then rolling down her sleeve, she said, "What about you? What do you do?"

"I go to school, Aunt Clare."

"I know that! What else? What about the clarinet?"

Then I had to bring out my instrument, put it together, and let her try it. "Owww!" she cried at the sound she made. She laid the instrument in its velvet case. "I was never musical." Then, leaning toward me as if I were about to tell her a spectacular story, she said, "What else, Phoebe? What else do you do?"

And I couldn't resist whispering my secret dream, telling her about the thing I longed for and feared. "Someday, I'm going to be a pilot. I'm going to get my flier's license."

"Fly? A flier? Oh, Phoebe." Her face opened, her huge dark eyes became even larger. "You'll fly like a bird!" She flapped her arms. "Your name is just right, after all."

That night she came into my room after I'd fallen asleep. I woke up—I must have sensed her staring at me—and saw her standing over my bed, a dark shadowy figure in the dim light from the kitchen. She wore a nightgown, and her hair, with that weird energy of its own, seemed to jump out in twists and snakes all over her head. Why was she staring at me? What was she thinking? Did she have a knife in her hand? Every horror movie I'd ever seen raced through my mind. Would my parents ever see me again? A thrill of pity for my helpless, lost-lamb self washed over me. I quivered beneath the sheet. "Amelia Earhart," I whispered. "Amelia Earhart!" And I made myself say, "What do you want, Aunt Clare?"

She was startled, took a step backward, muttered

something about pictures, and went out. After a while I fell asleep again. The next day I asked her why she had come into the room. "I just wanted to see you sleeping," she said.

"I don't like to be watched when I'm sleeping."

"Oh. Okay," she said reasonably.

Every day was the same as the day before. Hot, slow, dusty. I watched the weight lifter and carried on imaginary conversations.

Hello, down there.

Hello, up there.

My name is Phoebe and I'm a prisoner.

You mean that crazy woman?

Yes. She's got me locked in this terrible attic place.

Good grief. Phoebe! What do you want me to do?

Could you possibly walk up the side of the building with your fantastic legs so we could get better acquainted?

Other conversations didn't end so well.

Hello, Weight Lifter. You have nice legs and great pectorals.

Hello, girl-in-the-attic. What's your name? Who are you?

Phoebe. I'm visiting my Aunt Clare. You're cute.

You're cute, too, Phoebe.

Woo woo, want to get to know each other?

Sure, tell me all about yourself.

Well, my hero is Amelia Earhart.

Who's she, a model?

A flier! Everyone knows Amelia Earhart!

Oh, yeah? You know you talk crazy, just like your coo-coo aunt.

A few times I went down into the street and wandered around. Where I lived, the neighborhood was just houses with green lawns and Tarviaed driveways. But on this street, one next to another were little factories, stores, big rambly dusty houses, and little houses painted pink and yellow that leaned to one side and had tiny yards in which flowers and bushes grew in every inch of space. There were kids around, but I didn't know anybody.

One day Clare returned from work scowling and muttering to herself. "You," she cried accusingly, and for an hour she followed me around, commenting on everything I did. "She's opening the refrigerator. . . . She's taking out a bowl. Cold potatoes in the bowl. Putting the bowl on the table . . . Now she's eating from the bowl. She's chewing, chewing, chewing . . . She's going to the sink. . . ."

How furious I was with my parents! At that moment I hated them as passionately as I hated Clare. "Shut up," I cried.

Then an even stranger thing happened as she followed me into the bathroom. "Just ignore Clare," she advised me in a hasty whisper. And then, in the other voice, droning, ironic, "She's washing her hands. . . . She's rubbing them hard . . . putting on soap . . ."

Just ignore Clare. . . . As if she were two people, one caught in her obsessive detailing of my actions, the other an interested bystander full of helpful advice.

I'd always been aware of the strange people in the world, the ones I saw from the corner of my eyes. The old woman who patrolled the gutters for cigar butts. The man who barked like a seal from his front window. The two faceless old people who lived in a house so overgrown with vines you couldn't see a single window from the street. But those people had nothing to do with me. I had never liked to even think about them, and so I didn't.

But I couldn't "just ignore" Clare. I was in her house, sleeping in her bed, eating at her table, and listening to her strange noises. My chest ached. My parents had abandoned me to this crazy woman! For the first time, tears filled my eyes. Oh, Amelia Earhart, where are you when I need you?

I wrote my mother impassioned letters—"Can you come for me sooner than three weeks?" "I can't stand this anymore! If you leave me here, I'll be crazy like her." "She's awful, she's loony, and I hate her. Come for me right now!" Then I tore them up and wrote another letter. "How is Daddy? I think of you both all the time. I'm getting on okay with Aunt Clare. One thing you'll be glad of, she doesn't have a TV, so don't worry, I'm not sitting around just watching the boob tube."

A day or so later the landlady came knocking at Clare's door for the rent. "I see you have a visitor, dear." Mrs. Bidwell, fingering a stone necklace, stepped into the living room, looked carefully around and then coolly surveyed me from head to toe. Did she think I was crazy, too? She didn't come close to either of us. My head grew hot and I knew, just knew, that in a moment I might do something awful and rude, burp loudly or make other inexcusable noises.

"That's Phoebe," Clare said. "My niece—Mrs. Bidwell." Her voice was neither loud nor low, neither derisive nor apologetic. It was almost not a voice, but more the polite and right sounds and sentences that might come from a computer or a robot. And she stood like a robot, too, her arms stiffly at her sides.

"Must be nice for you to have company, dear," Mrs. Bidwell said, looking into the kitchen, then the bedroom. What was she searching for?

"Yes, it's nice for me to have company, Mrs. Bidwell. Here's the rent money, Mrs. Bidwell." Clare smoothed out the bills she took from the pocket of her orange Chinese-lantern skirt.

"All ready as usual. Your aunt is one of my very best tenants," she said to me with a gracious smile. "So neat and clean."

I smiled back like a robot. It was catching. Afraid to move, afraid anything I did, scratch my nose, scuffle my feet—anything at all—would look crazy to Mrs. Bidwell.

As soon as the door closed behind the landlady, Clare's face went into high gear. Her eyes rolled, she smirked and grimaced. "If I tell you something, will you keep it a secret? She's a *snoop*," Clare whispered hotly in my ear. "When I'm not here, she comes up and snoops *all over*."

"That's terrible," I whispered back.

"Don't—tell—that—I—know."

"I won't, dear," I said, mimicking Mrs. Bidwell.

"You're so sweet, dear," Clare responded with a gracious Mrs. Bidwell smile.

"And so neat and *clean*."

"The very *best* tenant," Clare cackled, and for the first time we laughed together.

That afternoon we began our marathon Monopoly game. "You want to play?" Clare said. Why not? It was something to do. She sprawled on the living-room floor, white legs waving in the air. I sat cross-legged, tending the money. The set was old, Community Chest and Chance cards all softly worn. We played all afternoon and left the game to finish the next day. But the next day we were still at it, and the day after, as well.

Monopoly with Clare was like no other Monopoly game in the world. She was so excited the entire time. She bought and sold feverishly, collected rents, built hotels, mortgaged properties, and crowed every time she collected two hundred dollars at GO. Our games went on for hours, for days, we began to eat supper while we played, and played after supper, forgetting the dishes. Monopoly came to be the center, the highlight, of my day. As soon as she returned from work, Clare said, "Ready?" Her feet danced. If I was eating, or rinsing a dish, she pulled me impatiently. "Come *on*, Phoebebird."

She was especially wild about the railroads. They were her favorite properties. If I had a railroad card, it drove her to passionate wheedling. "Let me buy the B and O from you, Phoebe. Phoebebird, Phoebebird, you can have *anything* of mine."

"Why do you want the old Body Odor Railroad?"

"Phoe*be*. I'm offering you good money!"

"Well . . . I'll think about it . . ." A moment later my Chance card told me to "Go directly to Jail. Do not pass GO, do not collect $200."

"You see! That's what you get for being stingy!" Clare put her fingers in her mouth and whistled. Sulking, I made my token, the man on the horse, drag his feet. Which made her laugh, big easy guffaws. *Whoop! Whoop! Whoop!* And I joined her, whooping, too, a new laugh, loud, free, crude.

The life I was leading with Clare began to seem realer than my "other life." I felt a loosening, loosening, as if I were a boat coming unmoored. It occurred to me that it didn't matter what I did, what I said. After a lifetime of being lovingly watched and supervised, I could walk around naked, pick toejam in the living room, or, if it suited me, eat nothing all day but pumpkin ice cream on white bread.

I stopped playing my clarinet, got up later every day, sometimes didn't bother getting out of my pajamas. I didn't wash my hair, forgot to brush my teeth, and looked blankly at the letter I'd been writing my parents for days, wondering how to fill the page. They were so far away, so distant.

"Of course, I had a boyfriend once," Clare said one afternoon as we played Monopoly. It was a habit of hers to start talking as if I knew what she had been thinking.

"Was he handsome?" I lay on the floor eating popcorn.

"Who?" Her hand hovered over Community Chest cards.

"Your boyfriend."

"Oh, Egbert! Phoebe! I was *pretty*—" She flung her head back. "I had to have a handsome boyfriend, didn't I? I called him Egbert Custard. Only he wasn't custard." She looked at me sideways. "He was very *tasty*." And she laughed. *Whoop! Whoop! Whoop!* Then, leaning across the board toward me: "After he went away, I used to say, 'Egbert, come *back*.' I'd talk to him. I'd tell him, 'I won't ask you all the time if you love me. I promise I won't. Come back, please, you could give me a baby and we'll be so happy.'"

Why had I never imagined Aunt Clare with a past any different from her present? Why had I thought of her only as "crazy"—as if that were a total definition of the shimmering, wavering, deep-water self that was Clare. "Didn't he ever come back?" I wanted a happy-ever-after ending.

Clare shook her head. "Let's not talk about it any-more!" But later that night she brought out a round, flowered tin box stuffed with photographs. "I'll show you my pictures," she said. "But you have to be careful. You hear me?"

"I won't mess them up."

"I don't mean that, you goose. Pictures can hurt you." She handed me a snapshot. "Be careful," she warned again. I took the picture under the light. There was my mother—young, grinning, wearing a sweat shirt and holding a baseball bat jauntily over one shoulder. I stared, amazed. Next, a picture of Clare and my mother sitting on the hood of a car, their knees crossed, arms behind them, each wearing peasant blouses pushed down on young shining shoulders.

"Here! Look at this one!" Clare was excited. A young man with sideburns, soft eyes, clasping a trumpet in his arms. "Egbert! Sweet Egbert!" Then another of Clare and my mother, and another, and another. Where was Crazy Clare in these old photos? Were her eyes a little shadowed? Her smile not quite so frank as my mother's? Did she hang back a bit more than necessary? I studied the faded pictures, hunting for clues to Clare and, yes, to myself.

My mother. My aunt. The words seemed mysterious, full of meaning. My heart pounded strangely. And a strange thought occurred to me—could not Clare have as easily been my mother as my mother?

I picked up another picture—the two sisters, one standing on each side of a slight man with a small dark mustache. My grandfather. He had died when I was an infant. "What was he like?" I said. "Grandpa—was he wonderful?"

Clare's eyes darkened, became that bottomless well. "He didn't like me." She snatched the picture from me, then scooped up all the pictures and shoved them into the tin box. "Why did you make me take them out?" she said accusingly.

"I didn't. That's *crazy*," I said.

Clare backed away from me, her long face closing down, collapsing.

"Aunt Clare, I didn't mean—"

She threw up her arms. "Go away."

"It was just—"

"*You said it.*" Turning, she pressed forehead and palms against the wall and stood there, rocking.

"Aunt Clare, come on."

"Go away."

"You want to play Monopoly?" No answer. "I'll sell you the B and O Railroad." No answer. "Let's sing some songs." (We had done that the night before, and I had taught her all my old camp songs.) No answer. "Clare, *please*," I said desperately.

"Go away, Phoebe." Dull voice, drowned in grief. I wanted to beat myself in the face for my stupid mistake.

"Clare, Aunt Clare—I'm *sorry*." So I was. Sorry for having hurt her; sorry for being thoughtless; and, not least of all, sorry for loving her and yet, somewhere inside me, still—still!—being afraid of her craziness.

I had seen her rigid and controlled with Mrs. Bidwell. With me she had finally trusted enough to let down the barriers—whoop with laughter and show me her pranky, unlatched self. Head to head, we had played Monopoly like two kids, or two adults—maybe just like two equals. Clare and Phoebe.

How mean of me, then, to tremble as I gingerly put my arms around her. To feel a frightened pounding in my stomach at the weight of her against my arms. There was not an ounce of the "dangerous maniac" in my Aunt Clare. There was not an ounce of nastiness or violence. She was odd—oh, yes, she was eccentric, she was not like anyone else in the world. But "crazy"? I no longer even knew what the word meant. The next day I made up with Clare. Two days later I was on my way home.

For a while everything seemed strange. I thought about Clare endlessly. My parents, neighbors, friends —all seemed so tight, squeezed-up, and dull. I had become accustomed to the Crazy Clare world where feelings showed on faces, adults said things like "liar" and "dope," danced when they were happy, and stood in corners in their despair.

A few times I began letters to her. "I miss playing Monopoly with you." "Be sure to give my regards to dear Mrs. Bidwell." "I have a new song to teach you." But my real life was taking me over. Friends. Music. School. My parents, my own room, movies and TV, and learning to play tennis. Friday nights were for washing hair, Sunday afternoons for rides in the country in our Willys Jeep.

My mother still called my aunt once a month. Oddly, Clare never asked to speak to me, nor I to her. Well, it really wasn't odd about me. I felt guilty, remembering my fear of touching her, my fear of *her*. And she—had she sensed that fear? Had she not forgotten my calling her crazy?

A year has passed. I hardly think of Clare at all anymore. Only, sometimes, I see a face that reminds me of her—it's the eyes, I think. And when it happens, all at once I'm overcome with longing to visit her, to lie on the floor and play Monopoly in my pajamas, to hear Clare whoop with laughter.

But then I think of those dark little attic rooms, and I remember how she stood with her face to the wall, and how she followed me around one day. *Now she's opening the refrigerator . . . taking out the potatoes . . . chewing them, chewing, chewing* . . . And I'm frightened. Yes, that's the truth.

Still, when I look into Amelia's brave flier's eyes, my heart marches, and I know that it doesn't matter about being frightened. *It really doesn't matter.* Being frightened is not the point. Not the point, at all. "Amelia Earhart, Amelia Earhart," I whisper, and then I know that someday I *will* go back to see Clare, just as I will, someday, fly.

How I Run Away and Make My Mother Toe the Line

My mother is Marlene Marie Victoria Thornton. I'm
Marlene Marie Theresa Thornton. My mother writes
letters to her sister in San Diego, California. At the
bottom she signs, "Love to Sister Ginny from your
sister Marlene M.V. Thornton."

Ever since I learned my letters I put my name down
on paper like this—Marlene M.T. Thornton. Wherever
I go to school—Rochester, New York, or anyplace, kids
say, "What's the *M.T.* for?" I say, "Marie Theresa."
They giggle, say, "No, it's for *empty!*" I get so mad
when they say that. I just get myself furious. I think,
Why did my mother name me such a stupid name! But
I don't stop signing Marlene M.T. Thornton on all my
school papers. That's my name.

I sign it in big letters. MARLENE M.T. THORN-TON. Sometimes a teacher says, "Very nice writing, Marlene." I tell my girl friend, Lucy, "Nobody better not say nothing about my name. 'Cause if they do, I sure will beat their butt."

Lucy laughs. "You can do it," she says.

Lucy is skinny and smart. I'm big and dumb. I know I am dumb. Once I hear a teacher say it. "That Marlene is a dumb kid. But you can't keep her back. Be like keeping a woman back." The one who says that isn't my teacher now, Miss Shelby. That teacher was in Rochester, New York. Sure glad I'm out of that city.

I had to live in Rochester, New York, for one whole year after my momma says she has had enough of *everybody*. First she kicks out my brother's father. That's Lonny Greenwood, my stepdaddy. Lonny Greenwood made my momma too mad, he made her just furious going with another woman. I feel sorry seeing Lonny Greenwood, my stepdaddy, a real nice man, going away. Next, my mean old momma sends my brother, Lance Vern Greenwood, to his grandmother in Washington, D.C. And then she sends *me*, Marlene Marie Theresa, to *my* grandmother in Rochester, New York.

My mother says she's going to live alone, get rid of all the leeches, and that's that! I was so *mad*. She didn't have to kick *me* out. My little brother, Lance Vern, he was giving a whole lot of trouble. Smoking, stuff like that. "Ten years old," my mother says, "and thinks he knows everything. Well, I've had it. You're going to your grandmother's, learn some respect, both of you."

So I go to Rochester, New York, and live with my grandmother Ruth. For one whole year I live with her in her house. Cute little house with a real attic, backyard, and everything. My grandmother just loves gardening, she grows great big flowers and the *best* tomatoes.

My grandmother, she could make some mean nasty faces about things, but she was a nice old lady. Didn't beat me or nothing, unless I did something so bad. Let me eat all the Pop-Tarts I wanted for breakfast. Never said I had to make my bed, except once a week I gotta put on clean sheets. But, still, all the time for one whole year I was saying to her, "Wish I could go back and live with my own sweet momma."

Every night before she ate supper, my grandmother put her teeth on the table. Put her spearmint chewing gum on top of her teeth. Then she'd turn on the TV news. Pretty soon she'd say, "The world is a nasty, ugly place, Marlene Marie Theresa." She'd watch some more news. House being bombed. Little kids stole away from their families. Poor men out of work. Pretty soon Grandmother Ruth is making her ugly faces. Looks just like a witch who could scare you. Whew! Every day I would say to myself, "Don't care if I *never* see one of my grandmother's ugly old faces again!"

I wrote my mother a letter. "You going to come get me? I got to look at Grandmother Ruth's teeth on the table every night. Watch her make ugly faces. She got whiskers, too."

Wrote my mother another letter. "I'm a real good girl. I never done anything wrong. I sure miss you. You are my own sweet momma. I'll be so happy to be gone from Rochester, New York. I just don't like this city." I signed my letters, "With love to my Dear Mother from Marlene M.T. Thornton."

One day my mother comes for me. She says, "Guess what, Marlene Marie Theresa? I got a new job, in a typing pool."

I think, What is a typing pool? I'm so dumb I think she means something like a swimming pool.

Momma says, "New job and new apartment. Isn't that something?" And she says, "Marlene Marie Theresa honey, you're going to come live with your mother again, baby. Back home where you belong." And she smiles at me and calls me Marlene Marie Theresa honey about one thousand times.

I sure was happy. Sure was dumb, too! 'Cause, guess what? After just a little time living with my momma, I'm so low and miserable feeling I could go right back and live with my Grandmother Ruth!

My mother don't let me do nothing. Can't go here, can't go there. Gotta come right home from school. Gotta do my homework. Every day she says, "You do your homework yet?" Yells all the time. Makes me do all the work in the house.

"Wash the dishes! Sweep the floor! Take out the trash!"

That's her special thing for me. Take out the trash! "Marlene Marie Theresa, did you take out the trash yet?" Every day, "Take out the trash." Why don't she take out the trash?

She says, "I'm working all day. I'm tired when I get home. You gotta do something for this household."

I say, "I'm doing *everything*."

She says, "Now you know that's not so. Who shops? Who cooks? Who pays the bills? Did you make your bed this morning?"

Every day I gotta make my bed. Why? Nobody sees it. Didn't make my bed at my Grandmother Ruth's. My mother says, Gotta keep the room clean. Gotta put everything away. "It's not nice to show your under-pants on the floor," she says. "Put them in the hamper. Hang up your blouse. Fold those socks together. Put them in the bureau." Can't leave nothing out or she yells at me like some old nasty witch.

I say, "Don't yell at me so much!"

She says, "Don't you bad-mouth me."

I say, "You the one with the bad mouth."

Whap! Slaps me right smack across the side of my head. I cry and do some screaming. Makes me so *mad* to be hit.

My mother says, "Oh, you're such a big girl and you're crying. You'll disturb the neighbors," she says. "You better stop that. People need their rest. Everyone works hard. Me, too," she says. "I am *so* tired. Just worn out."

She wants me to feel sorry. I just feel so mad. I think

how she always says, "Oh, my temper goes with my red hair!" But everybody knows she gets her red hair right out of the Miss Clairol bottle.

In my room I pull off all the covers I made neat in the morning for *her*. Throw them on the floor and wish I was back in Rochester, New York. I wipe my face on the pillow and wonder to myself, You gotta stay with your mother? No matter what? Is that a law?

Next day in school I ask my girl friend, Lucy, "You gotta stay with your mother? No matter what? Is that a law?"

My girl friend, Lucy, shakes her head yes. She is eight years old. My mother says, "Why are you friends with Lucy? You're twelve."

I say, "I like Lucy."

We walk to school together every day. Lucy don't bother me like other people do. I mean staring and all that. I got everything a woman has. Boys stare at my chest a lot. Diane is the prettiest girl in my class. I'm the biggest girl. I'm bigger than all the girls, bigger than most of the boys. Sure bigger than Miss Shelby. She's scared of me, giggles every time I ask her something. Why's she scared of me? I don't do anything to her. I try hard to learn. I don't want to be so dumb all the time.

Lucy don't have homework yet in her grade, so sometimes she helps me. Reads with me, helps me with the arithmetic problems, stuff like that. Lucy don't mind. She likes to help me.

Then my mother says in a mean voice, "You do your

own homework. You don't need an eight-year-old snot to do it for you. You're having trouble reading. Your teacher says you are not reading on a sixth-grade level. Do your own homework!" And she gives me a slap across the arm.

I say, "Why'd you slap me?"

She says, "Marlene Marie Theresa, you have to learn. You have to do your own work. Won't always be someone around to do it for you. *I want you to learn.* I can't watch over you every minute. You have to learn, and you have to be good!"

"I'm good," I say.

Then she says, "Did you take out the trash?"

Is that all she knows? Take out the trash! Do your homework! Clean your room! Cook the supper! She can think of one thousand things for me to do.

"I don't want you hanging around," she says. "There are a lot of bad boys around. You stay away from them. You study hard and you be good." She says working hard, doing my own homework, and taking out the trash gonna keep me from being bad.

I'm not bad.

I never do nothing bad till I run away.

What happened was, this one day me and Lucy decide we gotta have some fruit salad. "I want some fruit salad," Lucy says on the way home.

"Oh, me, too," I say. "I really want some fruit salad. Don't you, Lucy?"

"Yeah, I want some fruit salad so bad," Lucy says. "I can just taste that fruit salad."

We go to my house to make the fruit salad. My mother is still at work. There's a note on the fridge for me. The note says, "Marlene Marie Theresa, wash the kitchen floor. Scrub the sweet potatoes and put them in the oven. Set the table and get started on your homework." The note is stuck to the refrigerator door with a little magnet that looks like a teddy bear.

"That's a cute teddy bear," Lucy says. She pulls it off to look at it, and the note falls down on the floor. "Oh, oh, sorry," Lucy says. "I got your note all messed up."

"Well, who cares?" I say. "Just a stupid old note." And I say, "Marlene Marie Theresa, wash the floor," in this high funny voice. Lucy laughs. So I say, "Marlene Marie Theresa, put those sweet potatoes in that sweet potato oven." Lucy laughs some more. So I put my hands on my hips and I go all over the kitchen, wriggling, and saying how I should do my homework and all that, and Lucy almost falls down she is laughing so much.

"Oh, stop," she says, "I'm gonna pee my pants." And then we laugh even more. And we are still laughing when we open the can of Salada Fruit Salad. Looks *so* good, full of those little red maraschino cherries and grapes and all sorts of nice juicy stuff. I dump it in a big red bowl.

"You got any walnuts?" Lucy says.

"Sure," I say, " 'cause my mother just bought a whole bag full. She *loooves* walnuts."

"Walnuts taste wonderful in fruit salad," Lucy says.

We shell about half the bag and throw the walnuts

in the fruit salad. Lucy tastes the fruit salad. "Still needs something to make it perfect," she says. I taste the fruit salad.

"Tastes real nice to me," I say.

But Lucy says no, and we decide this fruit salad gotta have cottage cheese in it. We put in my mother's diet cottage cheese and stir it around.

"Now it tastes real, real *juicy*," I say.

"Well, I don't know," Lucy says. "Don't you want it to be *perfect*?"

"Sure," I say, so Lucy looks in the cupboard for something else to make the fruit salad perfect.

"I got it," she says, and she takes down a package of semi-sweet chocolate chips. She opens the package. I get a little bit worried. First my momma's walnuts, then her diet cottage cheese, and now her semi-sweet chips.

"My momma wants those semi-sweets to make cookies," I say.

"Oh, she won't miss a few," Lucy says. She dumps a whole ton of semi-sweet chocolate chips into the fruit salad. I grab the package out of her hand. Chocolate chips spill all over the floor. "See what you done," I say to Lucy.

"You done it," she says.

"You done it, you skinny string bean," I say.

"You done it with your big hands," she says.

We are both laughing like fools again.

"Clean it up," I say to Lucy.

"You clean it up," she says.

"You're smaller, so you do it," I say.

"You're bigger, so you do it," she says.

"Beat your butt if you don't," I say, and make a real ugly face like my grandmother's face when she watches TV news.

"Not afraid of you, Marlene Marie Theresa." Lucy sticks out her tongue. She knows I never touch her. I always say, Beat your butt, but I never touch nobody. Not afraid, just don't want to. I say to myself, Marlene Marie Theresa, don't hit nobody. It's not nice.

I rather hug Lucy than hit her. But I grab her anyway, just for fun, pretend I'm gonna make her clean up all those semi-sweets. She's a fast little booger, ducks away. We're pretending to fight, all over the kitchen. The semi-sweets are getting mushed by our feet. "It's a chocolate floor," Lucy says. "Yum yum!" We laugh so hard we sit right down on the floor, squash some more semi-sweets.

Right about then my mother comes home. Sees Lucy and me sitting on the chocolate floor. Sees walnut shells all over the counter. Sees her empty diet cottage cheese container. Sees semi-sweets rolling and squashed all over the place.

She starts screaming and hollering. "Marlene Marie Theresa Thornton, what are you *doing*? This place is a wreck! Are you going crazy? What is this mess?"

Lucy and me look at each other. My momma is screaming real loud, but we can't stop giggling for a second.

"Lucy, you get on home," my mother hollers. "Marlene, clean that mess up. Go on, Lucy! Go on, go on!"

"Don't bad-mouth Lucy," I say. "She didn't do nothing."

"Yeah, I did," Lucy says. "I spilled the chips on the floor, Mrs. Thornton."

"No, she didn't," I say.

"Yes, I did," Lucy says. "Mrs. Thornton, I did it."

"Both you fools shut up," Momma says. She shoves Lucy out the door, and smacks me hard three or four times, saying how I always make so much trouble for her. Then she runs to her room, slams the door.

I pick up chocolate chips. Think I'd rather see my grandmother's teeth on the table with chewing gum on top than be beat up all the time for *nothing*.

Momma opens her door and hollers some more. "That cleaned up yet? Marlene Marie Theresa Thornton, you better clean that up good! You better clean that up in a big hurry. I can't take much more of this."

I pick up some more mushy chips, thinking about Momma pushing Lucy. She shouldn't have done that to my girl friend. Just thinking about it is making me *so* mad. My momma's a mean nasty person. I kick some chips. Don't want to clean them up. Maybe I won't. It's her floor. She can clean up her own stupid old floor. Why's she always hollering and screaming and hitting on people? I walk out the back door.

I walk down the street. It's a hot night. Lotsa people out on their stoops and steps. Two dogs humping each other. Somebody is making something real good for supper. I smell hamburgers. Wish I had a hamburger. Keep walking. Cross the street. Go past the school and tell myself I'm running away.

That's good, I say to myself. You run away, Marlene Marie Theresa. You run away, make her sorry for being so mean.

I keep walking, down another block.

"Hey, Marlene."

I look around, see Diane from my class. "Hey, Diane."

"Whatcha doing?" she says. She's got big beautiful eyes.

"Nothing."

"Where you going?"

"No place."

"Uh-huh," Diane says. She's a medium-size girl. *Real* pretty. *So* pretty. She is *beautiful*. Wears her hair in lotta little pigtails. Wears a lotta little rings on all her fingers. She's on the porch of this old empty house. Windows all boarded up, stuff like that.

"Whatcha doing?" I say.

"Fooling around. Playing cards."

I look around. Don't see no cards.

"We're playing in there," Diane says. She means the empty house. "Want to play?"

"I don't know," I say. "Maybe." I'm leaning against a garbage can. Phew! It stinks.

"It's me and my brother and my cousin," Diane says.

"You got any food?" I say.

"Sure. Chips and soda and a whole bunch of Hostess Twinkies."

"You got any hamburgers?"

Diane shakes her head.

"Okay, I don't mind Hostess Twinkies."

We go inside. *Glad* to get away from that garbage can. "Gimme your hand," Diane says. It's dark inside. "You afraid of this house?"

"What for?" I say. "Just an old empty house."

"Oh, you know—some kids say it's haunted. They're dopes."

I give her hand a big squeeze. Wonder if she could be my second best friend, after Lucy.

They got candles in the kitchen and a table and some chairs. Diane's brother, Andrew, is tipping back on one chair. He's wearing a big straw hat. I say, "Hi." He says, "Hi." I don't know the other boy. He's John, Diane's cousin. He's cute. I say, "I'm Marlene Marie Theresa. You can call me Marlene." He gives me a cute look.

"How old are you, Marlene?"

I say, "Guess!" 'Cause I know he'll guess wrong.

"Bet you're sixteen," he says.

I say, "Yeah? I'm twelve years old."

He laughs like I said something so funny and gives me another cute look.

We play some cards. I eat two Hostess Twinkies. "Want some chips?" Andrew says. He's real nice, keeps giving me chips and soda and stuff.

Then John says, "You're sixteen, right?"

And I say, "Twelve."

And he laughs. "Oh, he, hem hem, he he." A real weird laugh. The more I say, "Twelve," the more he laughs. *Oh, he, hem hem, he he.*

Andrew says, "She's twelve. Marlene's twelve." He puts his straw hat on my head.

"That's right," Diane says. "She's twelve, just like me."

John laughs real hard, like we are all being *so* funny with him.

"Well, how old are you?" I say.

"I'm fifteen," he says. "Or am I eighteen?"

We are having such a good time. We play rummy and poker and eat all the chips and Twinkies. John says, "Who wants some beer?" He goes out and in a little bit comes back with a six-pack.

Andrew bangs down on his chair. "Where'd that come from?"

"I had it hid," John says. "Pretty snarky, huh? Hey, Marlene, let's you and me take some beer and go upstairs."

"Upstairs?" I say.

"Yeah," he says, "there's a real great mattress up there."

"Oh, you dirty buzzard," I say. And everybody laughs.

So then we're playing cards, and the boys are drinking beer, and me and Diane are taking sips. "Oh, um, this is *so* good," I say, but I don't like beer taste. Wish I had some more soda.

Andrew, all of a sudden, gets up and leaves, just

goes straight out the door. "Where's he going?" John says.

And Diane says, "You know old Andrew always gets sick when he drinks beers."

John says, "I forgot."

"No you didn't," Diane says.

"Not my fault if Andrew has a weak stomach," John says.

I say to myself, Marlene Marie Theresa, John knew Andrew would get sick. So then I don't like him so much anymore. And anyway, with Andrew gone, it's not so much fun. John is getting fresh with Diane, too, pulling her braids and grabbing her, and this and that, and a lot of stuff.

So Diane says, "I'm gonna leave. You're too nasty. You coming, Marlene?"

"Yeah, I'm coming," I say. "Can I stay overnight with you?"

"How come?"

"I'm running away."

John falls down laughing. "Running away," he says. "Oh, he, hem hem, he he."

"Why you running away?" Diane says.

" 'Cause my momma's so mean to me. Can I sleep over to your place?"

"You gonna make your momma toe the line?" John says. "Oh, he, hem hem, he he."

"Yeah, you can stay at my house," Diane says.

"I don't want Marlene to go," John says. He grabs my arm.

"Marlene wants to go," Diane says. She grabs my other arm.

"You stay, Marlene," John says. "We'll have some fun." He pulls my arm hard.

"No, I had enough fun," I said, "and I'm getting sleepy."

"Okay, let's go upstairs and sleep on the mattress."

"No, I'm going with Diane," I say.

He twists my arm. "You're staying."

"No, I'm not," I say.

"Yes, you are, 'cause I say you are." He is grinning. He's pulling one arm. Diane is pulling the other.

"No, I'm not staying with you," I say again.

"Yeah, you are." He gives my arm an extra hard twist. Burns it.

"Oh, you mean buzzard!" I pull my arm free from Diane and sock John in the stomach, sort of, but lower even. He goes, "Oh, uh," and gets this real weird, nasty expression on his face. Then me and Diane run out.

Diane's momma is already in bed. "That you, honey?" she calls. We're going up the stairs.

"Yeah, it's me, Mom," Diane says.

"Where've you been, honey? It's almost ten o'clock. Late."

"Just outside."

"Your brother, Andrew, came home early."

"Yeah, I know, Mom. I got a friend who wants to sleep over. Okay?"

"Okay, honey, but don't talk all through the night."

We go into Diane's room. Her two little sisters are already sleeping in the bunk beds. Diane and me get into her bed. I wish I wasn't so big. I get way over to one side. I don't want to take up all the place. "Your momma sounds real nice," I say.

"Yeah, she is."

"She ever yell at you?"

"No, not much."

"She ever beat you?"

"No."

We're whispering so we don't wake up her little sisters.

"My momma's sick," Diane whispers.

"What do you mean, sick?"

"She's got arthritis bad. It hurts her to do things."

I say, "Oh." I try to think of something to say to Diane to make her feel better about her momma being sick. After a long time I say, "Well, she's an old lady, anyway, I guess." But Diane doesn't answer, 'cause she's sleeping already.

I really like Diane's house when I see it in the morning. The living room is something. Beautiful red carpet on the floor, all the furniture polished, picture of flowers on the wall. "This is so nice," I say to Diane. "This is beautiful."

Diane and I go into the kitchen. "Let's have some French toast," Diane says. "We'll make it with cinnamon. Do you like jelly or syrup?"

"Jelly," I say, giving her my best smile. She is *so* nice. I beat the eggs and she gets the bread and jelly.

Diane's mother comes in, wearing a long green robe with a zipper. Just as pretty as Diane. She don't look sick to me. Not till I see her fingers, all bunched up and funny-looking.

"Now, who's this?" she says, smiling at me real nice.

"Marlene Marie Theresa Thornton," I say. "You can call me Marlene."

"Marlene Thornton," she says. "I thought so. Your mother is looking for you everyplace in the world, did you know that? You've got that poor woman scared to death."

Diane puts a big blob of butter on the pan. I don't say nothing.

"You better call your mother up, honey," Diane's mother says. "She was walking up and down the street last night asking everybody for you."

"Can I eat some French toast first?" I say. That French toast smells so good.

"Sure, honey. Want me to call her?"

I don't know if I do or if I don't. Diane's mother is looking at me like she wants me to say yes. I say, "Okay." I sit down and eat French toast with Diane. *Real* good. Then Andrew comes in and he wants some French toast. "Love it with cinnamon," he says. We start talking about playing cards and their Cousin John. "He sure is a mean buzzard," I say.

"Thinks he's so cute, too," Diane says.

Then Diane's mother comes back and says, "Marlene, here comes your mother down the street."

I get so scared I jump up out of my chair and run out the door. The sun is shining hard, and the sky is real blue. My mother sees me and yells, "Marlene Marie Theresa!" She comes right up to me. "Where have you been? You stayed out all night!"

"I'm running away," I say.

"You had me real scared. I didn't sleep all night."

"You're too mean and nasty," I say. I walk fast.

She walks right beside me. "Come on home," she says.

"I don't want to come home."

"Now, you know you don't mean that."

"Yeah, I do."

"Where you going to go?"

"I don't know. Someplace. Long way from you. You just scream all the time," I say. "Scream and beat me. Tell me I'm *bad*."

"Well, I'm tired from work," she says. "Chocolate chips all over the floor. No sweet potatoes cooking for supper."

I cross the street. She crosses the street, too. She takes my arm. "Come on home," she says again, and she starts saying *Marlene Marie Theresa honey*, like she did when she got me from my grandmother in Rochester.

"You just want me to take out the trash, work, all that stuff."

"I love you, Marlene Marie Theresa honey."

"Well, I don't know about that," I say.

"Yeah, I do," she says. "I really do. You're my first baby, honey." She gets tears in her eyes. That makes me feel *so* mean, but I keep on walking. Don't want to stop walking yet.

Momma fans her face. She's got lotta little bubbles of sweat on her forehead. "I really love you, baby," she says again. "Love you and your brother, Lance Vernon. Wish he was back home with us, too. Maybe in a few months we'll take a little trip to Washington, D.C., and get him. How'd you like that, Marlene Marie Theresa honey?"

I look at her sideways. She's smiling at me *so* nice. "Whew! It's a real hot day," I say.

"Oh, it surely is," Momma says.

"That sun sure is *hot*," I say. We pass the school playground. There's a fountain there right outside, near the school. I stop, take a drink. The water tastes real cool.

"This water tastes so good," I said. "Take a drink, Momma."

She takes a drink of water. "Oh, umm, this is *good* water," she says.

"Drink some more," I say, and I hold the handle for her. "Don't it taste good?" I say.

"Oh, this is the *best* water," she says. "Glad you told me to take a drink, Marlene Marie Theresa honey. This water is really fine."

We start walking again and we're holding hands and pretty soon we're hugging and kissing and all that stuff. I tell her about Andrew and Diane, and then I tell her about John. She gets so mad. She says she will march over to John's mother and tell her, "You keep your son away from my daughter!" She squeezes my arm and kisses me some more.

We go home. The kitchen is all cleaned up. House sure looks nice. No red carpet on the floor, but who cares. Momma has pretty little round blue and black rugs. Lampshade with a bluebird painted on it. Plants just filling up the windowsills.

"You hungry, Marlene Marie Theresa honey?" she says.

"No, Momma. Diane fed me good for breakfast. Gave me the best French toast and jelly. Real good."

"Okay," she says, "then what are you going to do now? Got all day Saturday."

"I don't know," I say. "Just fool around."

"Well, first take out the trash," she says.

I look at her. Can't believe my ears.

"Then you better wash the kitchen floor. I did it once, but it's still sticky from where you and Lucy messed around."

I look at her some more. Am I going crazy? Take out the trash? Wash the kitchen floor?

"And then you can do your homework," she says. "You don't want to get behind. You have to work hard to keep up. You have to work harder than some others."

"Oh, yeah," I say. I'm thinking, I gotta run away *again*?

Momma squeezes my arm. "My, didn't that water taste *good*, baby!"

"Yeah, it really tasted wonderful," I say.

Momma gives me another squeeze. "It was the *best* water," she says. "I'm *never* going to forget that water!"

"Me neither," I say.

Then I take out the trash.

Why Was Elena Crying?

When I was in first grade, my teacher, Miss Dooty, liked me—not just as well as she liked every other kid in her class, but maybe even more. Yes, the truth was, she did like me more, she smiled at me very specially, let me put my nap blanket near her desk, and often stroked my head as I passed by her into the room in the morning.

She was tall—she seemed very tall to me—with long, long slender legs and soft yellow skin and long black eyes. She wore pale mustard-colored suits in winter and pale, pale violet dresses that rustled in spring. To go to school in first grade was to enter a perfect world. Miss Dooty's world. Where I was liked *more*.

At home my parents liked me well enough, but they liked my sister, Elena, better.

"Why can't you be more like Elena?" my mother said once, exasperated at my tears over some trifle.

"I can't," I screamed, enraged at her stupidity, because of all the things I wanted in life, to be *more like Elena* topped the list. Oh, to have her large, moist, shining eyes instead of my little squinty green ones! Her thick dark hair instead of my frizzy head of curls! To have *her* temperament, *her* disposition, *her* cleverness, *her* ability to make people adore and love her! What was the *matter* with my mother? Didn't she know that if I could be more like Elena, I would, without question or hesitation?

Later my mother came into my room, when I was already half-asleep, and sat on my bed. "Carol . . ." She touched my head. "I'm sorry about what I said before. I didn't mean that, you know. You're fine the way you are. You're you, and I shouldn't have said that."

"Mmm." I bumped my head into her hip, nuzzling. I didn't blame her for what she'd said, and I didn't believe her now. It was nice of her to come and tell me I was fine, but we both knew better. I was a pain. A royal, tearful pain-in-the-ass.

No one ever said in so many words, *We like Elena better than Carol,* but there it was—something we all knew anyway. Just the way we knew that Max, our dachshund, our waddly hot dog, had a nasty habit of snooping through the garbage for the most disgusting putrid things he could find, which he would then snap down with satisfaction.

"Ugh, Max, you old disgusting thing," someone would say, at least once a day. Just as, to me, someone would be sure to say, "Carol, are you crying *again*?"

The *faucet*, they called me. The *leaky* faucet. My mother said if someone looked at me cross-eyed, I'd cry. It was true I cried more easily than anyone I knew and on all sorts of occasions. It was a thing I hated in myself, a part of me totally out of control. The moment I got the least bit excited, or sad, or worried, the tears came. My eyes filled, my nose stuffed up, I blubbered, and the tears ran.

I never thought it was wrong that my parents liked Elena more than me. It wasn't only that she never cried. She was also older, prettier, smarter, and, without doubt, a *much* nicer person. For instance, Elena helped my mother in the house without complaining, whereas I always grouched and moaned bitterly at the least suggestion of housework. Elena was fun to be around, she had a gorgeous smile, and she was generous with her things and about other people. On mornings after she had stayed overnight with a friend, and my parents and I were forced to share the breakfast table alone, all of us sighed and glanced around morosely, missing Elena.

Yes, Max was our garbage-hound, and I was our crybaby, and Elena—oh, Elena! Elena was our princess. That was what one of my uncles called her. "Hello, Princess," he'd say, and whenever he did, I seemed to see a kind of light shining out from her head and her hands. I did love Elena's hands; they were, like all her skin, the color of honey, and long and strong.

I don't want to give the wrong idea. Of course, Elena was normal—she also fretted over things, fought with me, and even annoyed my parents once in a while. But, for the most part, she was Elena, a shining special person.

And I was Carol, sometimes giggler, most often weeper and moaner. P.I.T.A. Pain-in-the-ass. I wondered that Miss Dooty could like me so much. She called me gigglepot. Her regard was a sweet, sweet mystery, and all that year I was in first grade, I hardly ever cried. Certainly not at all in school.

In second grade everything changed. My teacher, Chelia Woodenhead, did not like me *more*, or even a little bit better, than anyone else. That was all right at first, because Chelia Woodenhead seemed to be emotionless toward the whole restless lot of us. She spoke in a neutrally pitched, but firm, voice to everyone alike.

"Boys and girls, my name is Chelia Woodenhead. You will call me Miss Woodenhead. You will raise your hand when you want to speak. You will not leave your seats without permission."

Chelia Woodenhead was younger and prettier than Miss Dooty. She wore her hair down around her shoulders rather than pinned back in a knot as Miss Dooty had. She had a different pretty dress every day and even several pairs of wonderful tinted-lensed glasses, which she wore for marking our papers.

And then there was her mouth, like the rest of her—full, even lush and pretty. But when she wasn't speaking, this mouth was kept bitten together. I don't mean her lips were firmly pressed together, or that her mouth was set in a stern line. I mean her mouth was *bitten* together; there was a gathering and a puckering and a tightening and a tensing of her mouth, teeth, chin, and jaws that changed her whole face. I never knew if I was more frightened of her speaking or silent.

Well, there were her lips and the way she held them that I found terrifyingly fascinating, and there was her name, which I found deliriously funny. Woodenhead! I had only to say that name to myself, and the giggles would erupt. Woodenhead! The more I said it, the funnier it sounded. At home I said it to Elena, "Woodenhead!" and collapsed into fits of giggling. Elena joined in and both of us chanted, "Woodenhead! Woodenhead!" until Elena remembered she was four years older than I and ought to be more dignified.

All that first week in second grade, every time someone raised a hand and said, "Miss Woodenhead," I began to snort and sniffle, trying to cover my giggles.

And Miss Woodenhead began to pick me out from the other quieter, less erratic children. "Carol Wolpe, I do not think you're paying attention." "Carol, have you done your writing practice?" "Carol *Wolpe*, are you *giggling* again?"

. Miss Woodenhead's voice chilled me. It was a cold north wind that might have told the experienced or the wary that a storm was coming. Still in the summer dream of Miss Dooty's affection, still being *the giggle-pot*, I was unprepared.

"Miss Woodenhead," someone said. It was Friday afternoon. It was late. I was restless, dozy, dreamy, sleepy, giggly. I giggled.

"Carol Wolpe. What are you snickering about?"

"Uh, uh, uh," I said, trying not to laugh. "Uh, uh, nothing."

"Nothing, *Miss Woodenhead*."

"Nothing, Miss Woodenhead," I parroted, choking back another volcano of giggles at the sound of her name on my lips.

"How does one laugh at nothing, Carol?"

"I don't know."

"I don't know, Miss *Woodenhead*."

"I don't know, *Miss Woodenhead*," I repeated, the dangerous giggles still foaming at the corners of my mouth. Oh, silly Carol, swallow them back! Press your lips together! Make a mouth like Chelia Woodenhead's!

"Don't be smart with me!"

"Smart?" I repeated.

"I do not like children who mock me."

"Mock you?"

"Like *that*!"

"Like what?" I said. No longer giggling.

"Carol Wolpe. Come here."

I rose from my seat. I walked to the front of the room and stood in front of Miss Woodenhead.

"I will tell you once more. I do not like children who mock me."

My head swung back and forth. "I'm not mocking you." My heart, like my head, seemed to swing loosely, back and forth inside my chest. "I'm not mocking you," I bleated.

"*Use my name.*"

"Miss Woodenhead."

"Stand up straight! Now tell me—*what were you laughing about?*"

I no longer knew. Had I been laughing? Nothing seemed at all funny now.

"Speak up," she ordered.

I stared at her numbly. Speak up about *what*? I had lost the drift of this dialogue, had forgotten where, or why, it had begun. I was only, finally, aware that I was in dirty, dangerous waters. The rest of the class knew it, too. There was that kind of waiting stillness that comes over kids when one of them is in danger from a teacher. It's a stillness made up of relief that someone else is the target, uneasiness that at any moment the teacher might shift gears and attack *you*, and pleasure in watching another lamb being devoured.

Yes, that was exactly the way I felt by then, as if I were being devoured by the luscious lips of Chelia Woodenhead. I couldn't drag my gaze away from those lips.

"Look at me," she said. "Look me in the eyes!"

I did, but only for a moment, then *my* eyes dropped like a plummet to her lips, those lips. I felt compelled to watch them, as you might watch a pair of lunatic dogs, chained, but straining to reach you.

"You are a sneaky, shifty child, Carol Wolpe." This pronouncement was delivered in the same neutral tone of authority in which she informed us that two times two was four. A fact. A given. A piece of information without which we could not pass through second grade.

"Well?" Miss Woodenhead demanded.

What did she want now? What was I supposed to say? How act? "Yes," I said, thinking that might be safe.

"Yes, what?"

"Yes, Miss Woodenhead," I quivered.

"Yes, Miss Woodenhead," she repeated. "What does *that* mean?"

"I don't know," I said. "I don't *know!*" And I began to cry. I cried bitterly, without reservation, howls and wails of terror and outrage. There—at that moment— was where my crying career began again. After that, for years, so far as I can remember, I cried at every turn.

Of course, I was doomed in second grade. It was misery. So much misery that, as often as possible, I had a sore throat, a stomachache, a headache, or anything else that, by the grace of God, could make me an invalid for a day or two. And if I was very lucky and had been good (meaning no tears or storms for at least a day), my mother often let me spend those blessed, Woodenheadless days in Elena's room.

My room was bigger than hers, but hers was special. Tucked under the staircase to the attic, it had a sloping wall covered with faded wallpaper showing tiny ladies in blue ballgowns and tiny gentlemen in little white wigs and black ties dancing about with their hands daintily held in the air. I thought it was the most wonderful wall in the world, and if I stared hard enough at the tiny ladies and the tiny gentlemen, I would hear music and see them dance.

They took only the teeniest, tiniest steps, but they were all smiling and happy, and they said things to each other like, "Isn't it a dee-*light*ful day, Mr. Gorham-Atekins?" And "I do believe you are charming my heart, Miss Maxwell-Vandersniff."

Not only did Elena have Mr. Gorham-Atekins and Miss Maxwell-Vandersniff dancing perpetually on the wonderful sloping wall, but she also had a special window. Like all the other windows in the house, *my* windows were square, they had two panes of glass, they went up and down and sometimes they broke or cracked. Elena's window did all those things, too, but besides that it was set *into* the wall so that, instead of a window*sill*, she had a window *seat*. There was a cushion on the window seat, and to be allowed to sit there, reading, and eating a chocolate bar, on a rainy day was a privilege I rated only slightly below being asked to come into bed with Elena and tell her stories.

I had two basic kinds of stories in my repertoire—

ghost stories and love stories. Now this was interesting. *I* never cried when I told my stories, but Elena nearly always did, usually at the point where I either killed off my character (ghost story), or condemned her to forever roam the world (love story), always just missing her beloved. "Oh, how *sad*," Elena would sniffle. But things like that never drew a tear from me.

One year, in fifth grade, we were asked to write a composition on "The Most Wonderful Person I Know." I sat for five stricken minutes while, all around me, people bent to their papers. Then my hand went up. "Yes, Carol?" "Miss Clements—" My voice quivered, my eyes were wet. "I don't know who to write about." "Of course you do," she said briskly. *No, I didn't.* While I could make up stories easily for Elena, inventing fabulous happenings, school was different. School was *marks.* It meant being judged. It meant that cold snake in the center of my belly that had taken up residence in second grade and never left me. In school I didn't believe in myself, in what I could do, or that I could do *anything* praiseworthy. So, usually, I didn't do much.

My eyes swam. My nose twitched like a rabbit's. Then my friend, Bernie, poked me. "Write about your sister," she hissed. What relief. Of course! Elena *was* "The Most Wonderful Person I Know." I began, "My sister—" Simply writing those two words made my heart fill like a sponge absorbing water.

"Good for you!" Miss Clements wrote on my paper. "Why can't you always do work like this? Reminds me of your sister." All through grade school, junior high, and into high school, every teacher *I* had, had been *Elena's* teacher four years previously. And had not forgotten her.

"Wolpe?" the teacher would say on the first day. "Related to Elena Wolpe?"

"Elena's my *sister.*"

A nod, a smile, sometimes a congratulatory "Oh, very good, very good." After a while, I realized the teachers were congratulating themselves: they thought they were going to be lucky enough to have another Elena Wolpe in their classrooms. Instead, they got me.

I always started out the school year meaning to be like Elena, tearless, cooperative, smart, willing, and pleasant, but, somehow, before long, things became hopelessly fouled up. My teachers shook their heads. No Elena Wolpe, just another problem student.

"If only you'd try harder," Mr. Rideau, my eighth-grade history teacher, said to me once when I handed in a paper two weeks late.

"Yes," I said, my eyes filling, "*I will.*"

"But you told me the same thing weeks ago," he pointed out.

"I'll try," I said, blinking hard. Oh, please don't let me cry, I prayed. *Please.* "I'm sure I'll do better, Mr. Rideau." I fled before my traitorous tear ducts betrayed me again.

All my promises were given in utter sincerity. It was just that things happened. They happened *to* me, I felt, just as *tears* happened to me. I *meant* to do my work on time. I *always* meant to. I wrote down all the assignments and took the books home, but then, somehow, it was so *hard* to just sit down and do the work. Instead I'd roam around the house, playing with poor old Max (who was now half-blind), or I'd read for a while (always promising myself that at the end of *this* chapter I'd do my homework), or go into Elena's room for a chat with Mr. Goreham-Atekins and Miss Maxwell-Vandersniff.

That year—I was fourteen—Elena's life changed. She fell in love with Mark Feingold. Mark was in college on a basketball scholarship, he was an A student, he was tall and adorable with dark hair and a sweet, shy smile. He was, if anything, a male Elena. I immediately fell passionately in love with him.

Hopeless, of course. He brought me a gift. Crayons. *Crayons* for a fourteen-year-old! I was hot with despair. Those crayons—I couldn't bring myself to throw them away—but I seemed to read my future in them. I'd *never* find someone like Mark. Who would ever take me seriously? Who would ever want *me*, an endlessly leaking faucet?

Walking home one day, I heard, ahead of me, two girls discussing a third girl. They agreed that everyone liked this other girl. They did, too, but *why*? What was her magic? How did she attract and keep so many friends?

"She's so pretty," said one.

"Yes, but it's not that. Kathi is prettier. No, it's because she's nice to everyone."

"And not in a phony way."

"She always acts glad to see you."

"Yes, and not stuck up about how pretty she is and how much everyone likes her."

I *knew* it was Elena they were talking about. I rushed up. "Are you talking about Elena Wolpe?" They looked at me coolly. Who was this grungy little eavesdropper? "That's my sister." Now they looked at me again, differently. *This* is Elena Wolpe's sister? Elena, the beautiful and fair and good? They smiled cynically.

"She is, too, my sister," I shouted, and to my horror— but not surprise—my throat swelled, my eyes overflowed, and then I was *crying in public.* How I hated my tears! Despised them! Prayed to God night after night to make me a miracle, dry up my tears, turn me into a calm, tearless, radiant person like Elena.

I began to keep a calendar. For every day that passed tearless I crayoned in a large gold star. For every other day, an even larger, midnight blue, upside-down *T*. But it was my worst time of all. Worse, even, than second grade and Chelia Woodenhead. I could not get out of my head how *perfect* Elena was and how unperfect, flawed, and *hopeless* I was. I was miserable and so I cried. I cried rivers, lakes, oceans. If I woke up in the middle of the night, I'd think of Elena and Mark and cry. And in the morning, looking at my swollen eyes, it was all I could do not to cry again.

I *wanted* to stop crying. I not only hated my tears, I even hated anyone else's tears. In the movies if I saw a character crying on screen, while others around me sniffled sympathetically, I was overcome with disgust. I couldn't bear to read a crying scene in a book. I'd throw it across the room and refuse to read another page. But after only two months I tore up the calendar, sick of crayoning in only upside-down *T*s.

I tore each page of my calendar in half and then in half again, and then into confetti and threw it all over the floor. My mother passed my room. "What in the world—?"

"Never mind! Leave me alone!" My mother sighed and withdrew.

Then Elena came, carrying Max. "Carol, couldn't you be nicer to Mom?"

I tore up June. Bits of paper floated everywhere, settling on my bed, drifting into sneakers, mingling with the dust on shelves.

"What are you tearing up?" Elena said.

"You," I said, laughing maniacally so I wouldn't cry. "I'm tearing you up, Elena!" And I ripped July crosswise and then in half again and once more, and began on August. When I was done destroying the calendar, I broke every crayon into bits, and then threw myself across the confetti-covered bed and cried. I cried because I'd torn up my calendar, which I had really liked, cried because I had demolished Mark's gift, and cried because no one understood me. (Topping the list of people who didn't understand me was *me*.) And finally, of course, I cried because I was crying.

And I was so *tired* of my crying. So *bored* with my crying. Why couldn't I stop? I began howling like a dog.

"What's the *matter*?" Elena said, looking in again.

"Nothing," I howled. "Shut your face!"

She sat on the bed next to me. "Are you in pain? Are you sick?"

"Nooooo!"

"Carol, Carol . . ."

"I want to stop *crying*," I bawled miserably.

"Well, then," Elena said in my ear, "stop."

The logic of it! I sat up as if someone had whispered the secret of the universe. I shook my head like a dog, like Max when flies bothered him. *If you don't want to cry, don't cry. Stop.* It was such a revelation. It was as if, up until that instant, I had been living in a world where such thoughts were as unreal, as powerless, as Miss Maxwell-Vandersniff and Mr. Goreham-Atekins. *They* had to go on dancing eternally. And *I* had to go on crying.

I got up, looked in the mirror at my swollen eyes and dripping nose, and thought, What if I never cried again? It scared the hell out of me. What would I do instead? Pick my nose? Bang my head against the wall? *Anything*, I thought, *just stop crying*. And I remembered the five-mile cross-country run for the Children's Fund last year. The final mile had been torture. I had cried the whole mile, gasping for air, pushing one leaden leg before the other, but full of a stiff, sickening pride. I would *not* give up. I would *not* stop. I would go over the finish line, *running*. And I had. Now I felt the same sickening pride entering me. *I'll never cry again. I will not. I have stopped crying.*

A few weeks later at dinner, my father said, "I think the faucet has stopped dripping." I went on eating. Better not to talk about my tears or lack of tears. Better to just keep running that race. I did not cry for days, for weeks, for a whole month. Stars, stars, stars.

Then came the day when Elena and Mark told us they were going to get married. Everyone was hugging everyone else. Everyone was laughing and beaming and smiling. I, too, but it was my wide-eyed, wild-eyed grin against tears. *I wanted to cry!* Oh, for a good, long, satisfying sob. Oh, to throw myself across my bed and howl. Howl for the sheer luxury of it. Could one little crying session hurt that much?

I ran to my room. I threw myself across the bed. I pounded my fists into the mattress. I sniffled and choked. I was on the verge of tears, the way someone desperate might be on the edge of a cliff, ready to throw herself over. Why not crash? Did it matter? Who would care?

I would. I sat up, grinding fists into my eyes. *Oh, no, you don't. No-you-don't-Carol-Wolpe-Ex-Crier-Champion-of-the-World.* And I didn't.

The wedding was set for June, after Elena graduated. No big affair, just the family on both sides and some friends. Mark and Elena were writing their own vows and the ceremony would be held in our backyard. For weeks, nothing but the wedding was talked about in our house. "She is glowing," my mother said to a friend. "She is absolutely glowing."

But the night before the ceremony, I heard Elena crying in her room. Elena crying? Was it some weird trick of my mind? Now that *I* wasn't crying, *Elena* was? I knocked on her door. "Elena? It's me. Can I come in?"

"Yes." Muffled.

She was sitting up straight in her maple rocker, rocking and weeping. Sympathetic prickles began in my eyes.

"Elena?" I said. "Elena, what's the *matter*?"

"Oh, Carol!" She held out her arms and I fell down on my knees and hugged her. We stayed like that for a while, hugging and rocking, Elena weeping, crying as I had never heard her crying, and me trying like the devil to stay on the tearless wagon.

How scary it was to see Elena cry. I knew it had to be for some awful, secret, shocking reason. Was she dying of leukemia? I looked at her golden face, beautiful even covered with tears. No, she was healthier than all of us. Then had she discovered she didn't, after all, love Mark? For one instant I prepared to step into the breach. (Mark, will you marry me?) But then I thought of something even worse and nearly impossible to believe: *Mark* had changed his mind about marrying

Elena. What else could possibly have brought on such torrents of tears?

"Oh, Elena," I moaned, hugging her tighter.

"Carol, Carol—I'm—so—*scared*," she said.

"You'll find someone else," I said.

She stared at me and wiped her nose on a corner of her shirt. Elena, wiping her nose on her shirt? That was the sort of thing *Carol* did.

"You just wiped your nose on your shirt," I said.

"Why shouldn't I?" she said weepily. "You wipe your nose on *napkins*, for God's sake."

"I haven't done that for quite a while—"

"You scream and kick and rant and rave," she went on. "You think somebody's an ass, you *say* they're an ass."

"Not to their face," I said, ashamed.

"So *what*? You say it. Carol, do you realize I never say *anything* bad about *anyone*?"

"Of course you don't," I said. "That's why—"

"They all think I'm so *good*," she said.

"You *are*."

"Listen to me," she said. "*Listen* to me." She grabbed my arms. "I tell you I'm *scared*. Mark thinks I'm—wonderful." Her voice shook. "I love him so much, Carol. What happens when he finds out?"

"Finds out what?" I said in bewilderment.

"That I'm not *wonderful*."

"But you are," I said again.

"Shut up!" She sat up straighter. I shut up, never having been told to *shut up* by Elena. It just wasn't her style. "I always thought when I got older it would be different. I could just *relax*—be more like you—" My mouth fell open. Nothing came out. "—say the things I'm really thinking, not be so *nice* all the time. Nice, nice, they're always telling me how *nice* I am. I'm *not* that nice! No one is!"

I was stunned by the thought that Elena's perfection had been as much a burden to her as my crying had been to me. I wanted badly to help her, as she had helped me once. She had had the simple right words for me, but I couldn't think of a thing to say. So I just hugged her a lot more, until she said, "I'll be all right now, Carol. Thanks." I went back to my room. I wanted very much to cry, and I didn't.

The next day the weather was perfect. "Nervous?" my mother asked Elena at breakfast. She shook her head. She looked like herself again, at least the self I recognized.

So then, the wedding in our backyard. One of Mark's friends sang. My parents stood on one side of Elena and Mark, and his parents and his grandmother stood on the other side. I didn't hear too much of the ceremony. I was thinking about Elena, and I was thinking about me. About all the years behind me, and all the years ahead. About last night, and about tears and fears and other foul things.

When I looked up, Mark and Elena were kissing. They were married. My sister was a married woman. Elena, I thought, *Elena*, everything is changing.

A woman sitting next to me touched my arm. "Are you crying, dear? You're the sister of the bride, aren't you?"

"Yes," I said. "Yes, I am. *But I'm not crying.*" And indeed I wasn't.

Down Here on Greene Street

Lillian leans out the window watching Greene Street wake up. The morning shift of nurses, like white birds, are hurrying into the hospital, a big, sprawling red brick building, catty-corner from Lillian's house. Always something going on there. Down the block she sees that some old bum is sleeping in the doorway of the High Life Bar again. The sight makes her philosophical.

Down here on Greene Street I seen a lot, she thinks, and lights her first cigarette of the day. I seen men die and I seen babies born. This is a modest exaggeration. In the seventy years she's lived on Greene Street, she's seen one actual dead body and one baby born, when the parents didn't quite make it to the hospital and she happened to be right there on the street. But you never know, keep your eyes open, and you might see anything on Greene Street. And puffing on her cigarette, Lillian says vigorously, "Yeah, Greene Street!"

Really, she is thinking not about Greene Street now, but Fred Michel. Fred has certainly got a very red face, although after ten days she hardly ever notices it anymore. A nice, nice man. That's just what she told Raff, who only wanted to hear that Lillian is not serious about this idea of going to live with Fred in Florida.

"Don't do anything without talking to me first," Raff ordered.

"I got along a good many years okay on my own advice," Lillian says, waving her cigarette, practicing what she'll tell her daughter when she phones later.

A boy on a bike, with newspapers in a big canvas bag over his shoulder, pedals by. It's going to be another hot day. The sun already glints off the cars. Summertime sure isn't her most favorite time on Greene Street, but she can't complain. Here she is, seeing another summer, another day. And this early in the morning there's a nice breeze coming in the window.

If this was your ordinary day—but it isn't, Lillian reminds herself. Fred is coming over for lunch. She looks around the living room with a judicious eye, planning what she'll do to spruce it up. She's got the menu all planned. "How's this, Teddy Blue?" she says to the stuffed blue plush teddy bear sitting in the place of honor on the TV. "Deviled eggs, Parker House rolls, baked beans, sweet pickles, lemon Jell-O with bananas. And ice cream!" Some feast, Lillian thinks with as much satisfaction as if the meal were already spread out in front of her.

Usually in the morning after her chores, Lillian goes downstairs, sits on the stoop awhile watching Greene Street, then walks over to the elementary school where the city council put in a bench under a tree so mothers and so forth could sit down while their children play. There's a fountain there. There's swings, a slide, monkey bars, and so forth. It's a fine place to sit and Lillian enjoys watching the kids jumping around and screaming and brawling with each other. Her enjoyment is certainly one way Lillian knows she's not young anymore, because when her girls were kids, if they brawled, she wouldn't hesitate to cuff them both. A cuff for Rafferty, a cuff for Vera, always equal; she didn't favor one over the other. Back then her nerves couldn't stand fighting. Too much on her mind all the time. But now it's just fine with her to see kids picking at each other; all that energy, all that life—it just makes Lillian smile with pleasure. And if a mother gets too upset, Lillian will soothe her down a little, say, "Oh, they're just kids, it don't mean a thing, does it?"

Lots of times the mother will sort of smile with relief and just relax back against the seat. Lillian understands. No woman wants another woman to think she's a bad mother, can't control her kids or raise them right not to fight.

Sometimes Lillian gets into a nice little talk with the mother. Start on the weather (Hot day, isn't it?), then go to the kids (Hard work, but worth it), and after that, how the price of every living thing is going up every living day. Lillian certainly enjoys these little chats. "Just call me Lillian," she says, but sometimes the mother, who might be very young, even still a teen-ager, will say, "Oh, no, I couldn't." "Well, then, how about Mrs. Lillian?"

It comes out sometimes that Lillian lives alone and, even with two daughters, has no grandchildren. She always tries to give this information in her best matter-of-fact voice, and the same if the conversation gets around to Vera. Lillian's not, you know, looking for anybody's pity.

If her new friend is very, very interested, well then Lillian might tell her how, for eight years, Vera was going to come home for a visit, or Lillian was going to get in an airplane (for the first time) and visit *her* out there in Spokane. And she'll say how, you know, there was never enough money, or the weather was bad, or one or the other of them was sick. Not sick enough for alarm, just too sick to travel or have a visitor. Eight years she didn't see Vera. And then she gets a letter from a stranger telling her her daughter was dead. "Dear Mrs. Rouse, you don't know me, but I'm a friend of your daughter Vera . . ." How does a person, a beautiful young person you think is healthy and has the rest of her life to live, die so young and so far away from home and all of a sudden like that? Heart attack. They said it was a freak. Lillian never understood why her daughter's heart should stop working while *hers* would go on beating, strong as a horse, inside her chest.

Her park friend, hearing all this and full of sympathetic feelings, might pat Lillian's hand. Lillian's eyes will get wet. And it will all come over her again—the loss of her beautiful Vera.

And then later, sitting by her window in her favorite chair, looking down over Greene Street, cigarette in the corner of her mouth, Lillian likely will go into a daydream about Vera. Little Vera. Remember how women used to stop her on the street to say, "What a gorgeous child!" Rafferty was by no means a plug-ugly, but just didn't have a chance that way next to her little kid sister.

When Lillian thinks now of all the years, all the months, all the days and hours Vera and Rafferty lived with her, she's truly amazed at how little of it she remembers. Mostly it's snips here and snips there. Once in a dream she felt Vera's silky hair, felt it in her fingers and could still feel it when she woke up—those two little tangled, silky pigtails.

Lillian dreams about Raff, too, but not so much. She hopes she isn't playing favorites, but since she sees Raff one or two times a year when she comes up from New Jersey to visit, it's certainly different.

At the thought of Raff, Lillian coughs chestily. Raff

called her yesterday and would be calling again today, telling her, "Ma, don't do it. You don't know this man. And at your age—"

"Seventy-two isn't that old, Rafferty," Lillian says out loud.

"You think you'll go to beautiful Florida beaches," Raff had said. "They're all polluted. Full of tar, too. You can't even walk on the sand."

"I'll walk on the sidewalks, then, like I do here." *Now* Lillian has all the answers for Raff. Yesterday she listened and coughed.

In Florida she and Fred could walk together, listen to the radio, and watch the TV together: one night her favorite programs, the next night his. No more meals alone, no more sleeping alone, either. She won't say that to Raff, though—could just hear that little snort Raff gives when she thinks something is foolish. Raff is a lawyer—an amazing thing—went back to school when she was forty, and now she's a real lawyer. No kids.

Isn't it funny, Lillian thinks, how to a stranger you might sort of delicately hint around—was it by chance or choice that you have no children? But ask your own flesh and blood? Oh, no. Lillian has never come right out and asked Raff why no kids. In her heart Lillian is afraid that Raff will say she had no children because Lillian was such a poor mother.

I tried, I tried, I did my best, Lillian thinks, but she knows she did a lot of wrong things, such as filling her girls' air with cigarette smoke, and not always feeding them the very best good foods (sometimes so tired from working all day, she'd just heat up a can of beans, open a package of white bread). And what hurts her most is to remember hitting them for a least little thing. Not hard hits, but still, when she thinks of it now, it's real hurtful to her, brings on the bad feelings.

Okay, enough of that. Better stop this dreaming and get up and clean up her house. "Okay, Raff, I'm doing it," Lillian says, as if Raff could X-ray her eyes through the miles that separate them to see if Lillian is letting things go to pot. *That old dump*, Raff has said a thousand times.

No denying, this part of Greene Street has gone down somewhat over the years, the bar at the corner coming in and some of the houses getting real run-down, and the old Patterson place, that used to be such a big beautiful house always filled with snotty little Patterson kids, now torn down. And what goes up in its place, but a welding shop. Not what you would call high class. Even so, Greene Street, down its whole long winding length, is still a neighborhood place.

Raff has been after Lillian for years to come live with her and Martin in Teaneck. "You shouldn't live alone at your age, Mother." Well, now she's thinking about *not* living alone, and Raff is having lawyer's fits. Telling Lillian she's getting on, and what if she gets sick, and who is this man, and why is she so stubborn.

Lillian pinches out her cigarette carefully. She'll

smoke the butt later, cigarettes cost the world these days. "That's why I won't live with you, Raff," she says, getting up. "You hate it when I pinch a cigarette. Can't stand my smoking altogether. And another old thing, you'll want to put me on a diet, you'll tell me not to talk so loud, and I sure know we won't think the same things are funny."

Lillian checks the TV for her exercise program. Still a little early, so she starts the coffee going, wipes the counters, checks the mousetrap under the sink, and puts on eggs to boil. The ambulance shrieking down the street brings her to the window for a moment. After her babies were born, hearing that ambulance siren day and night gave her a real scared feeling that something would happen to her little ones.

"No, they'll be all right," Lenny had said every time. It vexed her. How could he say that? What did he know that she didn't? But he must have sincerely believed it, otherwise would he have gone off, good man that he was in his heart, and just left her and the two little girls? Eight years he was gone, and then he died of pneumonia.

Poor Lenny. She hardly ever thinks of him now. Her best reminder of Lenny had been Vera, who looked just like him. And then Vera died after being away from Lillian for eight years, too. That number eight sure makes Lillian nervous.

"How many letters in your name?" she asked Fred right after they met. And she counted his whole name. Fred (not Frederic) Michel. Ten letters. Four and six.

Also they met in July and on the fifteenth day. Now if it had been August, or on the sixteenth day (two eights) she would have worried.

It's time for her exercise program. "Arms *up*," comes the command from the TV set. Lillian throws up her hands, tries not to see the flesh trembling like Jell-O on her upper arms. "*Bend* from the waist. And touch those *toes*, ladies!"

"All right if I just go for the knees?" Lillian inquires. Exercising certainly makes her feel virtuous.

"Mother," Raff has said a million times, "it would do you a lot more good to lose some weight and give up smoking. Your lungs are probably in terrible shape."

"Oh, it's too late to start worrying now," she tells Raff. She never was one to worry a bone. So many things have happened over the years. All the little things—like Raff breaking her leg, and Lillian having to go on welfare that year she lost her job, and Vera flunking in school (even though the teachers said she was smart). And then the big things—Lillian's mother getting cancer, dying. Vera dead, age twenty-six. And Lenny, long before that, shooting out there to Arizona for his asthma and never coming back, always waiting for things to get better before asking her and the girls to join him. Just like Lenny to go off somewhere and have the bad sense to die alone.

She still has the letters he'd sent her. Ought to get rid of them. Maybe she would when she went to Florida. "Lillian, you and the girls are coming out as soon as I get the money together . . . and we'll have a house, a real house . . . and I'm going to buy you some bracelets and hair clips, silver hair clips." Who else but Lenny would say silver hair clips when she was busy figuring ways to put Silvercup bread on the table?

Lillian bends over, puffing. Raff was thirteen, Vera eleven, when their daddy died. Hardly knew him. They cried a little when she told them, then that was that. Raff seemed to cry just as hard about the boozums she didn't have yet.

"Raff, honey," Lillian would tell her, "this family, we're slow developers. Look at me *now*, and I didn't have one little anything till I was eighteen." A small exaggeration, what you might call a white lie, but it made Raff feel better.

"You sure?" she would say, giving Lillian a look from those dark eyes, big round brown eyes, just like Lillian's own.

"Sure, I'm sure," Lillian would say, giving Raff a big hug. When they were about three or four and started talking was when Lillian got to really like her girls. She liked a good conversation anytime, and once she could talk person-to-person with Raff and Vera, she was certainly amazed. Those little peanuts had good sense, especially Raff; you just had to look into her brown eyes and you knew that one knew the score.

Vera, now, was altogether a different type, more the dreamy type. Looked like her father and was him all the way through—blondie, blue eyes, knock you dead with her looks, but didn't give a fig about that, all caught up in her dreams.

Just like Lenny, Lillian thinks, jumping heavily up and down and clapping her hands over her head. Ooof . . . Ooooof . . . That Jack LaLanne is something else, is he really in his sixties? Some men never looked that good in their twenties. She likes a man who takes care of himself, that's one thing she noticed right away about Fred. Every day, clean socks, clean shirt, *and* a clean handkerchief in his breast pocket. Classy.

"Michel, used to be Michlowitz," he told her pretty soon after they met. "My father got it changed by the immigration when he got off the boat."

"This is a very nice man," she told Raff. "Clean, and honest." That honest part, especially, ought to have appealed to Raff, who didn't ever mind hitting you over the head, so long as she hit you with the truth.

"He's six years younger than you," Raff said.

"Five," Lillian said, right back.

"Mother! You know what I mean." Forty-seven years old, and sometimes Raff still says *Moth*-er like she did when she was fifteen. And every time she says it that way—*Moth*-er—Lillian somehow feels all used up. Funny how your own kids can get you feeling worse than anybody. Why should that be?

"And a final vigorous jog in place to get that heart going," the TV reminds her.

"If you don't mind, Jack," Lillian says, "I'll pass."

Anyway, shaking the bathroom rug out the window is good exercise, too. On the street the kids are starting to come out. A girl is bouncing a ball, flipping her leg over it as it rises.

"Hello, Marla, hello, Donna," Lillian calls down.

"Hello, Mrs. Lillian. . . . *A* is for Annette who is Always Awful. *B* is for Barbara who is a Busy Brat. *C* is for Celia who is a Curious Cookie. *D* is for . . ."

Lillian pulls in the rug, remembering, Oh, *Greene* Street . . . *mean* street . . . black *bean* street . . . Funny how you never forget some things.

Coughing and humming, she cleans up the rest of the apartment, moving so fast she forgets she's a fat old lady. Might very well be twenty, twenty-five years younger the way she's feeling just then.

By the time she hears Fred's knock at the door, everything's done. She gives a last look around, folds a newspaper, and puts it on the TV next to Teddy Blue. "Coming," she calls. Everything looks fresh and nice. She's certainly satisfied. The table is set for lunch and she's wearing a fresh-ironed blouse over her slacks, and a green bead necklace. However, what with the heat and rushing around to clean, her feet got swollen, so she's not wearing shoes. She hopes Fred doesn't mind.

That's the first thing she says. "Do you mind bare feet?" And shows hers. They're clean, he can see that.

"Why, that's Florida feet," he says, and the joke starts things off just right.

She admires the way he looks. He's wearing a light blue shirt, neat trousers, sandals. "Well, come on in," she says, even though he's in already. Amazingly, this is the first time he's been here. Every other day they've met on the street, gone to the playground to watch kids, or just walked around, talking.

She leads him around the apartment, maybe showing off a little, you know, how she's fixed everything just so—her pictures of the girls, her little knickknacks and things she's gotten here and there. "All this is my own. Everything you see here I worked for," she says, and thinks of those years working in stores and shops and factories. She didn't quit till she was sixty-nine and Raff insisted. Sure, it's a comfort not to have to get up in the morning, but sometimes she still misses working.

"Just this guy here. I didn't *work* for him." She points to Teddy Blue. There's a starched blue ribbon around his neck. He looks brand-new and he's— what? Thirty-five, thirty-six years old? "That's my little friend," she says. "He's a story and a half."

Fred smooths back his hair, which is slick and silver, just beautiful, and leans in toward her, all ready to listen. "You want the short version or the long of the short?" she says to make him laugh. Then she tells him about that day she and the girls went to the carnival on Bing Street. She'd been saving all her change in a glass jelly jar so as to give the girls a good time, give them every ride, and they just went helling from one thing to another. Couldn't tell who was moving faster or enjoying herself more, her or the girls.

Then she saw Teddy Blue in a shooting gallery and fell in love with him, just had to have him. She knew how to shoot, definitely did. Used to rat-hunt in the dump with her big brothers. She went all out for Teddy Blue. "Didn't take me that many tries, either," she can't help boasting.

Fred is very much surprised about the shooting, but she can see that everything she says is making him like her even more, maybe because she's getting him to see her thirty, thirty-five years ago. The real fine part is that, as she talks, *she* sees herself all those years ago, pulling Raff and Vera around by the hands, and raring to go.

"I'll call you Annie Oakley from now on," Fred says, and they're both jolly when they sit down to lunch. It's certainly nice to have someone to eat with. She doesn't mind a bit! Good that he smokes. Nothing worse than being with one of those no-smokers, always waving their hands in the air, and pretending to cough to make you feel guilty for enjoying your little pleasure in life.

"Isn't it something that we never met before," she says, not for the first time.

"And I come up to visit my son every year," he says, also not for the first time.

"Today makes ten days," Lillian says.

"It does, indeed," says Fred. "I noticed it on the calendar."

And with the greatest of pleasure they go over once again all the little details of the day they met. "It was hot," Lillian says.

"But raining," Fred reminds her.

"But not that much," she says. "It didn't keep me in."

"My good luck," Fred says.

She had been on the way to the Piggly-Wiggly market for a quart of milk. Fred—she didn't know it was Fred then, of course, just noticed that he had quite a surprising red face—Fred stopped her and asked directions to the same market. And he was going to buy a quart of milk, too. That was some coincidence! "Just follow me," she had said, but then, of course, they'd walked along together and discovered that every year he came up to visit his son, who lived right around the corner from Greene Street on 6 Elm Street. Well, here was another coincidence—her house number was 6 also. Naturally, they introduced themselves.

In the Piggly-Wiggly she showed him the dairy case, they got in line together to check out, and he gave her the green stamps although she said maybe his daughter-in-law saved them. But he said he wanted Lillian to have them.

The next day, what do you know, there he was right outside her building. Just happened to be walking past, he said. Only later told her he'd been walking past about half a dozen times, hoping she'd come out. They had a terrific laugh about that. And another one when she told that she'd been on the lookout for him, too! Every day after that they met to walk and talk. But they're sure not talked out yet.

"So you've always lived here on Greene Street?" he says.

"All except for two years. And right here in this same apartment for fifty years."

"Well," he says, "I and my wife never lived in one place more than five years."

Lillian shakes her head in amazement. "Is that right! And me fifty years in one place. I bet that could go in the *Book of World Records*. I'd be famous then."

"One of my grandsons is a little famous," Fred says. "He's a producer of TV documentaries. He got an Emmy one year for a show on wild horses."

"Isn't that something!" Lillian certainly enjoys this news. She'll have to remember to tell Raff.

After lunch Lillian and Fred sit by the window, smoking and looking down at Greene Street together. "It's a lively street," Fred says.

"Hardly ever a dull moment," Lillian agrees.

"There wouldn't be around you," he says. A siren wails. "Here comes the ambulance. You'll be glad to hear the last of that. You don't hear that where I am."

Lillian watches the ambulance turn into the hospital drive. She nudges Fred with her shoulder. "What do you think of this—my daughter is still rubbing it in that we met without being introduced."

He smiles. "Children have their own ideas."

Lillian nods. "Isn't that the truth. Want another

coffin nail?" She feels comfortable with Fred, just real comfortable.

"This is a nice apartment," he says, taking the cigarette. "You fixed it up, you have a touch."

"If I say so myself," Lillian agrees with a modest smile. Must be he's talking apartment to lead up to what's on both their minds: when will she come down to Florida? He's leaving tomorrow.

Just as if he read her mind, he says, "It would be nice to have everything settled. I'm all packed, you know."

"Already!"

"I don't travel with that much. One suitcase. I wash my things out every night. You learn that when you're a traveling salesman."

"I do the same," Lillian says, "even though I never traveled." She thinks of their socks and underpants hanging companionably next to each other over a shower bar. "You know," she says, "this Florida thing is a big decision to make." It certainly is a shame Fred needs to live in Florida for his heart. If he lived up here with his son, she and he could see each other, visit back and forth. And maybe some other things, too. She isn't that old.

"Florida is a beautiful state," Fred says in a coaxing voice.

"Oh, but the summers are awful," Lillian says wisely.

"Well, I have air conditioning, and right nearby is a nice swimming pool."

"I'm too fat to get into a bathing suit."

"I like the way you look. My wife was built something like you, and she had a good sense of humor, too."

She doesn't mind that he talks about his wife, and compares them. Shows he's a sensitive person, a human being with feelings. She wonders, Would he want to sleep in separate beds? "Do you like a double bed or singles?" She comes right out with it.

Oh, how he laughs, and blushes like a boy, right up to his ears. His red face gets redder still. "Double," he says. Fine feelings are certainly coming over Lillian now.

When he leaves later, Fred squeezes her hand and says, "I'll come by in the morning. My plane goes at three."

Lillian nods. She promises that, by tomorrow, she'll have a date picked for her departure. She kisses him on the cheek. Then they put their arms around each other and kiss a long kiss, full of many sweet and fine feelings.

When Raff calls that evening, Lillian tells her, "I might be leaving in a month."

Raff is silent for a moment, then says, "You're really going to do it?"

"It certainly looks that way."

"Well, then, I wish you luck, Mother."

"Thank you, Rafferty." It's a dignified moment.

In bed, Lillian lies awake for a long time thinking of

all the things to be done. Will she store her furniture? No. Give it away. There isn't much of it worth anything. But worn and shabby as her things are, it hurts to think of them falling into the hands of strangers. She can't make up her mind what to do and falls asleep wondering if there's a nice place to sit and chat with the young mothers where Fred lives.

In the middle of the night Lillian wakes from a sound sleep and bolts out of bed as if someone on Greene Street—or Greene Street itself—is calling her. What was it? Why did she wake up?

The street is quiet for a change. Light spills from the window of the bar, more light from the dimmed hospital. A couple, arm-in-arm, hurries down the street, heels clicking. Lillian watches them until they are out of sight, thinking of Florida, where she's never been, and of Greene Street, which she's hardly ever left.

She's unable to get back to sleep. Something feels unfinished. Hardly thinking about it, she gets dressed, puts on her shoes, and, for reasons unknown, takes Teddy Blue as she goes out the door and quietly down the stairs.

She walks down Greene Street, Teddy Blue tucked under her arm, past the mostly dark houses, past the dimly lit hospital, past more houses, the welding shop, dark parked cars, a man walking a dog. They told you not to go out at night, especially the senior citizens, but how could she feel afraid on Greene Street? Past the bakery, the smell of new baked bread lingering, then on past the elementary school, the dark playground, the benches, and the fountain. Walking, just walking on Greene Street.

The night air is cool and moist. She thinks of Vera, and it comes to her as if it had just happened that her grown-up baby daughter, her once little girl, her youngest, sweetest, and ever willfullest child, is dead. And Lenny is dead. And all her family are gone, her parents and her brothers. And Raff lives in New Jersey. And she's old, seventy-two, old and fat and has nothing left in the world but Greene Street itself.

She walks for a long time. It's getting light in the sky when she goes slowly back up her steps. In the apartment she lies down with her clothes on, a hand on her forehead. Her heart is shaking and she wonders if she is going to die.

Later she gets up and showers. How tired she is, how heavy-limbed. She squeezes toothpaste onto her brush. She is proud that she still has all her own teeth, but this morning she thinks not of that, but of the liver spots on the back of her hands.

The sun is coming up hot again. When Fred knocks at the door, she moves slowly to open up. "Paper boy!" he says, holding out her newspaper. He looks fresh in his Florida shirt of many colors. She makes coffee and they sit by the window, where she tells him about her midnight walk.

"Alone? You went alone?" He shakes his head.

"Oh, I had Teddy Blue with me," she says.

"Your protector. I hope you'll bring Teddy Blue along."

He is joking, but she says seriously, "I wouldn't leave Teddy Blue behind." She rubs the arm of her chair, the once velvet nap worn down from use. This is the chair into which she always sinks with a sigh, happy or sad, depending on her life events of the day, to watch out the window at Greene Street.

Fred remarks that she seems quiet and after a while asks if she has settled on that departure date. Lillian shakes her head. "I still have to mull it over." She leans out the window. Car horns honk; a motorcycle roars by. The air has lost its freshness, is woven thick with sound.

"Cigarette?" Fred offers.

"I'll just take a puff of yours." She then surprises herself by adding, "I might decide to give up the weed altogether."

"That would be all right with me," he says, but he looks doubtful.

She hands the cigarette back to him. Not to smoke would be as strange as being in Florida. Strange and foreign land. Would she die in Florida? Would she die of lung cancer? Or would she be one of the lucky ones who smoke and get away with it? She had always thought she would die on Greene Street, and maybe right in that same bed she's slept in for fifty years.

The morning goes by in little bumps and starts. "You have my address and phone number?" Fred says.

She shows him where she'd written it down on a pad, right next to the phone. "And you'll let me know your plans? This is a good time to fly, because the fare isn't so expensive."

When it's time for him to leave, Fred kisses her. She kisses him back and rubs her nose into his skin. He smells good—shaving lotion and a clean soapy smell. "Well, good-bye for now," he says.

"For now," she echoes to his retreating back, and then she begins to feel again all the alarming symptoms of last night: a heavy, dull tiredness, and her heart shaking as if it wanted to burst out of her chest. "Oh," she says. "Oh! I'm afraid my heart won't stand it!" And in the moment of saying it she understands that to leave Greene Street, even for Fred, might very well break her heart.

From Florida, Fred sends her postcards. She sends him funny stories clipped from the newspaper. They both look forward to his visit to his son the following year. From time to time he phones to ask if she has changed her mind. They smoke as they talk and cough at each other over the wire. It's their hearts, Lillian says. His heart won't let him live on Greene Street; hers won't let her leave.

"It's our foolish hearts," she says. The way she says it is like a song, and indeed there is a song called "Your Foolish Heart." One day on the radio she hears an old recording of Jimmie Rodgers singing that song. Lovely, she thinks, letting the tears rise, oh, *lovely* the way he sings. Just makes you want to cry.

For My Father
Who Died, Etcetera

———————————

I would like to write a poem
For my father.
This is the way it would start:
For my father who died, etcetera.

I would like to write a story
About my father.
This is the way it would start:
This story is about my father
Who lived an ordinary life.

On a shelf I keep his glasses.
Books held to his nose he read, he read.

———————————

"I'm reading War and Peace," he said.
"It's the fourth time."

He was a milkman, a breadman—
"I'm a route man," he said.
World War Two, he worked in Alco—
Fat times. $125 a week.
"One-hundred-twenty-five dollars," he said,
"Let me see that check again."

He died choking for air
Strangled in a hospital bed—
Asbestosis.
Shipyard workers get it,
So do their families
Sniffing the dust in their clothes.

Hey, he was a route man
How come he died like that?

On the feeder, a cardinal, orange bill dipped in snow.
"Look at that bird," he said
As if he saw more than a blood-colored blur,
"Look at that bird, beautiful winter bird."

Once he pushed a broom
In a little tin-roofed factory,
Unpacked crates of asbestos.
"Only a couple weeks," he said,
"Two, maybe three weeks."

He died choking for air.
First of course he slowly got weaker—
One day he fell down in the street.
His sister had chemotherapy and died anyway.
"I hope my hair doesn't fall out," he said.

He died choking for air.
"Get the ticket," he said, "I'm taking the ship."
Months later I saw him—
(It was a dream of course)
I on a balcony, he below.
"Excuse me, Dad" (I was polite)
"Don't want to hurt your feelings,
"But you're supposed to be dead."